"Welcome to Cape Diablo."

The man's tone didn't match his words.

"Thanks. I'm Jaci Matlock, the new tenant."

"Yeah, I know."

So this was the caretaker. He didn't look that bad for a recluse who'd spent half his life on a secluded island. He was as unfriendly as she'd expected. She'd have to play this just right to get him to talk to her about the past, or even let her into the boathouse.

"Follow me," he said.

An icy tremble slithered down Jaci's spine as she started up the shadowy path toward the house. The crimes might have occurred thirty years ago, but the air seemed alive with dark and possibly deadly secrets.

The situation was a forensic student's dream, unless...

Unless it turned into a nightmare.

JOANNA WAYNE

A CLANDESTINE AFFAIR

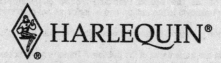

HARLEQUIN®

TORONTO • NEW YORK • LONDON
AMSTERDAM • PARIS • SYDNEY • HAMBURG
STOCKHOLM • ATHENS • TOKYO • MILAN • MADRID
PRAGUE • WARSAW • BUDAPEST • AUCKLAND

To Amanda Stevens and B.J. Daniels who, as always,
were a ball to work with. And a special thanks to Denise Zaza,
our wonderful editor, who puts up with all three of us
and whose editorial insight and guidance is invaluable.
And, of course, to all of you readers who help us keep
writing the stories we love by buying our books
of intrigue, passion and happy endings.

ISBN-13: 978-0-373-88716-3
ISBN-10:   0-373-88716-7

A CLANDESTINE AFFAIR

This edition published by arrangement with Harlequin Books S.A.

® and TM are trademarks of the publisher. Trademarks indicated with
® are registered in the United States Patent and Trademark Office, the
Canadian Trade Marks Office and in other countries.

www.eHarlequin.com

Printed in U.S.A.

ABOUT THE AUTHOR

When not creating tales of spine-tingling suspense and heartwarming romance, Joanna Wayne enjoys reading, traveling, playing golf and spending time with family and friends.

Joanna believes that one of the special joys of writing is knowing that her stories have brought enjoyment to or somehow touched the lives of her readers.

Books by Joanna Wayne

*Hidden Passions
†Hidden Passions: Full Moon Madness

Don't miss any of our special offers. Write to us at the following address for information on our newest releases.

Harlequin Reader Service
U.S.: 3010 Walden Ave., P.O. Box 1325, Buffalo, NY 14269
Canadian: P.O. Box 609, Fort Erie, Ont. L2A 5X3

CAST OF CHARACTERS

Jaci Matlock—The cold murder case is just a project until she becomes obsessed with finding the truth about what happened that murderous night on Cape Diablo thirty years ago.

Raoul Lazario—He'd expected a challenge when he came to the island to see Carlos, but he wasn't prepared for Jaci Matlock or the danger that threatened her.

Mac Lowell—He is the investigating officer who'd made detailed photos of the crime scene and blood splatters the night the Santiago family had disappeared.

Bull Gatlan—The man who delivers visitors and supplies to Cape Diablo.

Enrique Lopez—Friend of Carlos and Alma, but his interest seems to lie in seducing Jaci.

Ralph Linsky and Jack Paige—Detectives from Everglades City.

Carlos Lazario—Raoul's great-uncle, a friend to Andres Santiago and caretaker of Cape Diablo. A man with secrets of his own.

Alma Garcia—She'd been the Santiago children's nanny until they'd disappeared. Now she's delusional and wanders the island in a tattered white dress.

The Santiago Family—Andres had run a smuggling operation and built the once-beautiful Spanish villa that dominates the island. Medina was the daughter of a fallen Central American dictator and Andres's second wife. Their two daughters, Pilar and Reyna, disappeared alongside them thirty years ago.

Chapter One

Jaci Matlock could look at crime scene photos by the hour and never once get bored. But after a half hour in a Naples, Florida, art gallery with her mother, she was all but climbing the walls. Even the flute of bubbly the gallery owner had pressed into her hand didn't help, though she'd have hated to face the evening without it.

Her mother stopped in front of an abstract that looked as if it had been painted by a menopausal chimpanzee. She stared at it for a minute. "I hate to imagine what the artist was thinking when she painted that."

"Another night of reruns?" Jaci offered.

"Or when will my daughter come for a real visit?"

"I'm standing right next to you. That feels like a real visit to me."

"Two days and one night is not a real visit. Are you sure you can't stay longer?"

"If I did, I'd be rambling through the house alone. You're leaving for a month's cruise Wednesday."

"You could use a vacation yourself. We could go to Europe for a couple of weeks when I get back, just the two of us. Paris is lovely in the fall."

"Or we could have lunch at that new French restaurant you were telling me about. I can possibly spring for the tip."

"I'm not kidding, Jaci. You spend far too much time wallowing in the morbid. Clarence and I could give you the trip as an early present for earning your graduate degree."

Her mother's husband, Clarence Harding III, could definitely afford it. And to give the old fart credit where credit was due, he was generous with his darling wife, Evelyn and Jaci as well.

But Jaci was far too independent—and stubborn—to live on her stepfather's handouts. Thankfully, her father had started a college fund for her before he'd died. That, a part-time job waiting tables and the small inheritance she'd received from her dad's parents had let her earn her undergraduate and Master's degrees with a minimum of loans.

Almost. She still had one major hurdle to pass.

"If I don't complete my thesis project this semester, I won't be getting the degree," she said, omitting the fact that spending two weeks stalking Paris boutiques with her mother would be far more punishing than any assignment Professor Greeley could dream up.

"I know you have your paper to write, but surely you could work on that just as well in Paris."

"It's not a paper. It's a project." They'd had this conversation before, and if her mother didn't consider forensics an F word instead of a science, she'd have remembered that.

Actually, the project should already be half-finished, but Jaci had run into a major complication. After six years of literally getting away with murder, the killer in her research crime had found religion and confessed to everything.

The family of the slain woman was thrilled

to have closure. Jaci was back to square one as far as her project was concerned. Not a lot of hypothesizing she could do on a case that was solved by the killer's confession, and she hadn't found another cold case that spurred her interest the way that one had.

"Oh, look, there's Mrs. Baxter and her son, Matthew. He's a surgeon," Evelyn crooned. "Nice looking—and single."

Which meant her mother had dreams of matchmaking dancing in her head. Jaci sized up the guy as he approached with an over-weight, middle-aged woman dripping diamonds. He was Caucasian, just under six feet, medium build, dark hair, lighter mustache. No visible tattoos or distinguishing marks.

She groaned silently. Maybe she had spent too many hours buried in evidence. Actually, the guy was cute, but then so were beagles. Dogs required a lot less energy than a relation-ship, and she didn't even have time for them.

She half listened while her mother and Mrs. Baxter exchanged greetings, then met Matthew's eyes briefly when her mom made the introductions. Jaci put out her hand, and from the second his closed around hers, she was mesmerized—by the painting hanging just beyond his right shoulder.

"It's the Santiago house."

Matthew let go of her hand. "Excuse me?"

"That painting," she said, walking around him to stand in front of it. "It's the house where the Santiago family was living when they disappeared."

"I'm sorry. Were they friends of yours?"

"Not likely. I wasn't even born when they went missing."

"My daughter's studying to become a forensics scientist," her mother said, almost apologetically.

"That's interesting," Matthew said. "How did you choose that for a career?"

"It kind of chose me." She didn't bother to explain; her attention was focused on the painting. She barely managed a "nice to meet you" when the surgeon and his mother moved on.

"You certainly scared him off fast enough," Evelyn said. "I'm assuming that was your purpose in fawning over that macabre painting."

"It's not just a painting. That's the house on Cape Diablo."

Her mother stepped back, tilted her head slightly and studied the picture. "What's Cape Diablo?"

"One of the mangrove islands off the coast. It's not that far from here."

"The bougainvillea looks as if it's bleeding all over that decaying villa. It's repulsive."

So were the facts. A wealthy but scandalous drug runner, his wife and two children had disappeared from the house and the island thirty years ago. The only clue to what might have happened to them was splattered blood found in the boathouse.

The crime had fascinated Jaci since she was eleven and had heard her father and his partner talking about it one night when they'd thought she was asleep.

"I can't imagine why an artist would want to create something so morbid," Evelyn said.

"That's nothing compared with what you hear and see on the nightly news."

Her mother put her hand on Jaci's shoulder. "You are so much like your father."

The hint of melancholy in her voice surprised Jaci almost as much as the mention of her father did. He'd been dead eleven years and they'd been divorced for three before that. Her mother probably hadn't mentioned his name a dozen times since the divorce, and never since his funeral.

All Jaci had known of the facts surrounding the divorce was that it had broken her dad's heart. It had broken hers, as well. And Clarence Harding III's entrance into the picture so soon after hadn't made matters any better.

Jaci stepped closer to the painting and studied the artist's signature, "W. St. Clair." It was almost hidden in the trunk of a mangrove in the bottom right corner of the canvas.

Her mother had already moved on. Jaci joined her in front of a painting of a blue heron perched on the bow of a sinking sailboat. "Are you familiar with the work of W. St. Clair?" Jaci asked.

"No. Is that who painted that horrid picture?"

"Yes."

"Then I don't plan to become familiar with his work."

His? Maybe. But Jaci had the feeling the painting had been done by a woman. She wasn't sure why.

"Do you have a pen?"

Her mother fished a silver ballpoint from her Prada handbag and handed it to her. Jaci scribbled the artist's name on the napkin she'd been holding under her champagne glass, then slipped the napkin into her skirt pocket as she returned the pen.

"You surely aren't thinking of buying that painting," her mother said. "The house looks as if it came straight from a nightmare."

"On my budget? Are you kidding? I'm just curious about the artist. But the Santiago disappearance would make a fascinating subject for my culminating project. And it's nearby," she added, thinking aloud more than making conversation.

"You wouldn't actually visit Cape Fear, would you?"

"Cape Diablo, Mother, and there's no reason not to go there. It's a nice quiet, secluded island amid ten thousand others in the Gulf of Mexico."

"I don't like it. In fact, I'm getting a really bad feeling about the place."

So was Jaci. It was probably the crimson paint splattered like fresh blood. But she was desperate for a project, and the murder case was still as much a mystery as it had been thirty years ago.

Besides, there was nothing to fear on the island—nothing but isolation and an aging mansion that likely held deadly secrets hidden within its crumbling walls. All within an hour of the mainland by a fast boat.

The night hadn't been a waste, after all.

FOR THE NEXT TEN DAYS, Jaci ate, slept and breathed the Santiago murders. She was so engrossed in the details, she half expected old Andres Santiago to be standing by her bed when she woke up in the morning.

But who knew what might happen when she actually reached Cape Diablo? She was headed there now, booked into one of the small apartments in what had once been a lavish pool house, or so said one of the many articles she'd read on the Santiagos' disappearance.

She'd tried to reach Wilma St. Clair and had finally tracked her down to a residence in South Dakota, of all places. But the artist was out of town on her honeymoon and there was no way to reach her.

Jaci had also tried to get in contact with

Mac Lowell, the cop who'd taken the detailed pictures of the blood splatters on the boathouse wall the night the family had disappeared.

That was a wash, as well. He'd quit the force right after that and moved out of the area. He'd later inherited his mother's Everglades City beach house and went to visit on rare occasions. Jaci was still hoping to contact him.

She'd left word with the neighbors and also stuck a note beneath the door, asking him to call her—covering all bases in case he made a trip back to the area.

His partner that night was also unavailable. He'd been killed in a car crash about the same time Mac had moved away.

The good news was that once Professor Greeley intervened on her behalf, the Everglades City Police Department had released copies of the blood splatter photos and the pertinent police records.

The bad news was that other than the photos, the police reports left a lot to be desired. Crime scene investigations from thirty years ago, especially when the crime involved a smuggler's family living on an island that hadn't fallen under the jurisdiction of a big-city police force, didn't even approach today's standards.

Jaci swatted at a mosquito that was circling her in search of a target not coated in insect repellent. "How much farther?"

Bull Gatlin kept his eyes straight ahead. "Another ten minutes or so."

She hoped the trip wouldn't take longer than that. It was already dusk, and she didn't want to be out in these waters with nothing but the moon and stars to light their way.

She didn't see how the pilot could find Cape Diablo as it was. One island followed another, all looking pretty much the same: swamp grasses, sand, jungles of mangroves that grew along the edge of the water.

Walking trees. That's what her dad had called the mangroves when he'd taken her fishing out in the gulf. The tangled red roots made the spindly trees look as if they were walking on the incoming surf.

Jaci settled back into the memories. At age thirteen she'd been certain losing him was the end of the world. She still missed him, especially on nights like this when she could all but hear his deep, rumbling laugh and see the sweat trickling down his brow below the grungy old hat he'd worn on their fishing excursions.

He'd considered himself an ordinary cop, but she'd be happy if she could be half as good at locating evidence and solving crimes as he'd been.

"You plan to stay long?"

The boatman's question yanked her back to the present. "I'm not sure."

"You brought a lot of luggage."

"Only four bags and my laptop."

"That black duffel could hold enough for a year-long stay. Felt like it, too, when I put it in the boat."

So what was he—the luggage patrol? The duffel contained her research material, and that was none of his business. "I won't be staying a year."

"Bet not. Most folks don't stay more than a few days."

"Why not?"

"Not much to do there. No TV. No entertainment 'less you like to fish, and you need a large boat to do that right, one you can take out in the open waters of the gulf."

"No distractions. No demands. That's the beauty of a secluded island."

"Cape Diablo's secluded, that's for sure. I'm the only one who goes out there regularly, and that's only 'cause I get paid to do it. Last man who had this job was murdered right there on the island."

"When did that happen?"

"About three months ago. Pete got mixed up with some crazy broad who went around killing people for the fun of it. That's the kind of folks you get on Cape Diablo. Woman like you won't stay long."

If his plan was to give her the creeps, he was succeeding. She studied him while he steered the boat through one of the narrower channels. He was scrawny with blond scraggly hair that fell a couple of inches past his collar.

Maybe forty. Maybe not. Hard to tell, since his face showed the signs of too much sun and not enough sun block. Looked pretty much like your basic beach bum, but his name had been given to her when she'd made the rental arrangements.

"Do you run a regular shuttle to Cape Diablo?" she asked as he slowed to maneuver through a narrow spit.

He rubbed his fingers through his unkempt beard. "I bring mail and supplies out twice a week. Occasionally I make an extra run to transport a tenant."

"Only an occasional tenant?"

"Yeah, but then I've just been on the job a few months, and we've had a run of bad weather this year, tropical storms popping up like mushrooms."

"Mr. Cochburn said I should call you if I need supplies from town."

"Mr. Cochburn told you that, did he?"

"Yes, he's the attorney I talked to when I made the rental arrangements."

"I know who he is. I just don't see why he doesn't level with folks he's sending out here."

"Then you don't deliver supplies?"

"I deliver them, all right—mail and supplies twice a week, like I said—but good luck trying to call, unless you got one of them satellite phones. Other than that, cell service is about as dependable as a FEMA roof in a hurricane."

Jaci hadn't considered that possibility. "What do people on the island do in case of an emergency?"

"Tough it out. Guess that's all part of the beauty of having no distractions," he said, clearly mocking her earlier optimism. "That's it up ahead. Not much to see this time of the night, but the house is pretty impressive if you arrive by day, especially while you're too far away to see its dilapidated condition."

The narrow dock they were approaching was lighted, but beyond that all she could see was a tangle of tree branches and one light shining from the top of a rambling Spanish villa.

"That's the old woman's apartment," Bull said, as if reading her mind. "Surely Mr. Cochburn told you about her."

"He didn't mention any of the tenants."

"She ain't a tenant. More of a permanent fixture, and crazy as they come, that one." He circled his finger by his right temple to make his point. "Spent too much time sniffing the white stuff, if you know what I mean."

"Are you talking about Alma Garcia?"

"Yeah. So you do know about her."

Absolutely. Jaci knew about Carlos Lazario, as well. In fact, they had been the deciding factors for her moving onto the island instead of just hiring a boat to take her out for a day.

Alma had been the nanny for the Santiago family. Carlos was said to have been Andres Santiago's right-hand man and bodyguard. Reportedly neither Carlos nor Alma had been on the island at the time of the disappearance, but they were now, thirty years after the fact.

Jaci was eager to talk to them, but didn't plan to tell them why she was here. Better to let them think she was just a tourist in pursuit of a little R and R. It would make snooping easier.

"Carlos, the old caretaker, he's been here forever, too," Bull said, surprisingly talkative now that he'd gotten started. "He's all right, but don't mess with him if you can help it. He's tired of tenants. Says all they do is cause trouble. Seems like that's true of the ones he gets out here. Me, you couldn't pay me to spend the night. They got bogs out in that swamp that can suck you in and bury you in the mud quicker than you can sing a chorus of 'Margaritaville.'"

Another little problem Mr. Cochburn had failed to mention. "Thanks for the warning. I'll make certain to stay out of the swamp."

"Yeah, and I guess you know there's no electricity out here except for a generator. You can hear it running all over the island, kind of a constant low drone. Gotta be some kind of dark at night if it ever goes off."

The wind picked up and Jaci pulled her light jacket tighter while Bull docked and tied up the boat. He helped her out, then unloaded her luggage, dropping it on the edge of the dock.

She stood for a moment, soaking up the atmosphere. Every crime scene she'd ever visited had its own feel about it. Cape Diablo was no different, except that her instant reactions to the place were even more pronounced than usual.

The island had a sinister aura about it, as if the place itself might hold evil. More likely she was letting the seclusion get to her. A good forensics expert wouldn't be influenced by that, and neither would she. But first impressions did matter.

A gray-haired man stepped into the clearing near the dock, a black Lab following a step behind. For a second it seemed that the man had appeared from nowhere, but a closer look revealed a slightly overgrown path that led back to the boathouse. The two-story structure was at the edge of the clearing, just as described in the police report. Only the reports had not mentioned how spooky the run-down place looked in the deepening grays of twilight.

"Welcome to Cape Diablo." The man's tone didn't match his words.

"Thanks. I'm Jaci Matlock, the new tenant."

"Yeah, I know."

"And that's Carlos Lazario," Bull said.

So that was Carlos. He didn't look that bad for a recluse who'd spent almost half his life on a secluded island. He was unfriendly as she'd expected. She'd have to play this just right to get him to talk to her about the past, or even let her in the boathouse.

Carlos scanned the pile of luggage. "All this?" he asked, shaking his head.

"I tend to overpack," she said, tossing the laptop over her shoulder and picking up the two smaller bags. "I can carry my own luggage," she said. "I'll come back for the rest."

"I'll bring 'em," Carlos said, "but don't go expecting me to wait on you." He turned to Bull. "Did you get my order?"

"I got it right here."

"Good."

Bull reached inside an old cooler at the front to the boat and took out a package wrapped in brown paper. "It wasn't easy to come by," he said, handing it to the man.

"I appreciate it."

"You be careful, Carlos. You don't need any trouble at your age."

"I'm not going looking for any."

The verbal exchange between the two men bordered on the surreptitious, and Jaci would have loved to know what was in the package.

Carlos tucked it in the pocket of his tattered black jacket, then bent and picked up the two heaviest pieces of luggage with seemingly little effort. He was strong for a man his age.

"Follow me," he said.

"Sure you want to stay?" Bull asked, climbing back into the boat.

"I'm sure."

But an icy tremble slithered down Jaci's spine as she started up the shadowy path toward the house. The crimes might have occurred thirty years ago, but the air seemed alive with dark and possibly deadly secrets.

The situation was a forensic student's dream, unless...

Unless it turned into a nightmare.

Chapter Two

Alma stood near the edge of the courtyard
watching the new tenant as the young woman
completed a series of lunges and squats. Her
skimpy black running shorts revealed long,
tanned legs, and a white jogging bra
stretched across her perky, ample breasts.

Even with no makeup, and her auburn hair
pulled through the back of a baseball cap and
flowing loose behind her like a horse's
mane, Jaci Matlock was striking.

But then, it was easy to be striking when
you were Jaci's age. Mid-twenties, Alma
suspected—young, but still older than Alma
had been when she'd first come to Cape
Diablo.

She had been striking, too, though she
would never have dressed in such scandalous
attire. She'd worn white peasant blouses and

full cotton skirts that only revealed her ankles when the fabric was billowed by ocean breezes.

Her hair had hung to her waist, straight and black as onyx. Her complexion had been flawless, always carefully protected from the sun by large-brimmed straw hats woven by her grandmother back in their tiny Central American country.

Her face was gaunt now, her once flawless complexion weathered and wrinkled until she was only an unrecognizable shadow of the beautiful young woman she'd once been. Even her hair had betrayed her, lost its gleam and become wiry and prematurely gray.

When Alma had first come to the island, she'd missed her family and friends terribly. Worse, the isolation had frightened her. The wind whispering through the branches of the trees had reminded her of the wailing of women whose husbands and sons had never come home from battle.

But Cape Diablo had been the pathway to her future, the awakening of her dreams. Dreams that had withered and died almost as quickly as the seaweed that washed up on the beach to bake in the noonday sun once the tide had receded.

All because of the events that had transpired one dark night.

The secrets were old and tattered now, threadbare like her white festival dress. And yet they ruled the island like angry demons. The spirits dwelled in every crevice of the crumbling mansion, and had seeped between the tiniest grains of sand.

"Beware, Jaci," she whispered as she backed into the shadows beyond the courtyard wall. "The curse of Cape Diablo shows no mercy."

CARLOS PULLED THE WORN fishing hat low on his forehead as he squinted to read Raoul's letter for the second time that morning. The note hadn't come by regular mail delivery. His late brother's only grandson never used the post.

Instead, it had been hand delivered by a courier who'd arrived by speedboat while Carlos was checking his stone crab traps. He'd read it and stuffed it in his pocket while he finished emptying the night's catch.

Carlos reread the note now, carefully this

time, to make sure he had not overlooked Raoul's arrival date. But no, it wasn't there. All he'd written was that he was coming for a short visit.

But he would arrive soon, possibly tonight. Raoul never gave a lot of advance notice for his rare stopovers at the island.

Carlos folded the note and stuck it back in his shirt pocket, grimacing as he did. The last time Raoul had been to the island was to tell him that Raoul's grandfather had died. He'd come and taken Carlos back to the mainland to pay his last respects to his only brother.

Emilio's death had hit Carlos much harder than he'd expected. Not that he'd seen him much over the last thirty years. Emilio had never understood the ties that bound Carlos to this place after the terrible tragedy, and Carlos hadn't dared explain.

Feeling torn between his desire to see his great-nephew and his concern for what might have prompted the unexpected visit, Carlos left the shade of the mangroves and walked across the sandy beach behind the big house.

Courtesy demanded he let the *señora* know that Raoul was coming, though he wasn't sure she'd recognize Raoul or realize he was Emilio's son. She seemed confused about a lot of things these days—another source of worry for him.

Occasionally a tenant questioned him about the old woman who stared at them from the third-floor window, or from behind the courtyard wall, yet avoided talking to them even if they encountered her on the beach.

Carlos merely shrugged when they asked, refusing to offer an explanation. The *señora* belonged to the island and the house. The vacationers were the intruders, and he had had nothing but trouble from them over the last few months. The visitors had become more deadly than the drug smugglers who'd always used the island for their nefarious business.

And now there was a new one. Jaci Matlock. She seemed nice enough, but there was an intensity about her that worried Carlos. Not that she'd asked many questions when she'd arrived last night. It was more the way she'd scrutinized him when he'd carried her things inside the apartment. And the way she'd stared at the villa, as if she was making notes in her mind.

Or maybe he was just growing paranoid in his old age. He was seventy-three and felt it in his joints and bones. Nothing like the days when he'd been strong and daring, fighting for his hero right up until General Norberto was killed and his dictatorship overthrown.

The old memories set in, more comfortable in his mind than thoughts of Raoul or the island's new inhabitant. The sun grew hot on Carlos's back as he walked. Even though it was mid-October, the heat penetrated his thin shirt as if his skin was bare.

The heat didn't really bother him. He'd grown used to it years ago. The sun and the island were like old friends, he thought as he paused to watch a blue heron step along the shore, searching for its breakfast.

Carlos's heartbeat quickened as he spotted something that looked like a human bone bobbing around in the retreating tide. He waded in and slapped both hands into the water. On his second try, his fingers closed around the wave-tossed object.

Driftwood. Only a piece of driftwood.

He stared at it for long minutes, then flipped it back into the water. Paranoia was definitely setting in.

"Good morning, Carlos."

He jumped at the sound of his name, and turned around to find Jaci Matlock standing a few feet away. He had no idea how long she'd been there, or if she'd seen him frantically groping for the driftwood, only to return it to the churning waters of the gulf.

"Good morning, Miss Matlock."

"The island is even more beautiful and peaceful than I pictured it. And the villa is fascinating."

"It's a crumbling relic."

She bent to pick up a sand dollar that had washed ashore. "Your traps were full this morning."

"How do you know?"

"I saw you empty them."

"Then you must have been up with the sun."

"I'm an early riser."

"I didn't see you on the dock."

"No. I was on the beach, using my binoculars to watch a couple of dolphins frolic."

But at least for a while her binoculars had been focused on him. Paranoia or not, his suspicions about her presence on the island grew. "How did you find out about Cape Diablo?"

"My mother suggested it. She lives in Naples, and apparently some of her friends vacationed here. They raved about the quiet, secluded beach and the marvelous view of the gulf. They also bragged about the crabs. May I buy a few from you? They'd make a nice dinner."

"I don't supply food to the tenants."

Tamale came running up to join them, going straight to Jaci. She knelt in the sand and he jumped excitedly, licking her hands and face.

"Come along, Tamale," Carlos said.

"Tamale, what a neat name for a dog."

"It's just a name. First thing that came to mind when some guys dumped him from a boat a few yards from shore and never came back for him. That was almost a month ago."

"Lucky for Tamale. He seems at home here."

He walked away, but Jaci joined him, her willowy shadow dancing with his plumper and slightly stooped one. The silence rode between them until they'd almost reached the cutoff to the overgrown garden and the arched opening to the courtyard.

"How long have you lived on Cape Diablo?" she asked.

He looked at her for a second and met her

penetrating gaze before glancing away. "Too many years to count."

"You must love it to have stayed so long."

"It's home."

"I'm interested in seeing the villa. What time are the tours?"

"Tours?"

"Yes, Mr. Cochburn said you give tours of the villa to tenants staying here. Actually, I tried to rent one of the apartments inside the big house, but he said they were closed temporarily for repairs."

"I don't know what Mr. Cochran told you, but there are no tours."

"Then perhaps you could show me around."

"No. The villa is off-limits to visitors at this time."

"Because of the damage from recent storms?"

He nodded, though her assumption was false. The villa had become too dangerous over the last few weeks and the tenants too upsetting for the *señora*. "I must insist that you not enter the villa during your stay."

"That's disappointing."

He expected more argument, but she skipped ahead for the last few yards, kicking through the surf and playing chase with Tamale like a small child. Her mixture of innocence and intensity left him more confused than ever about her reasons for coming to Cape Diablo.

She stopped when she reached the overgrown garden surrounding the courtyard, and stooped to pick a late bloom from a bush all but strangled by a lush crop of weeds.

When Andres had lived here, there had been enough servants to keep the house and gardens in impeccable condition. It still saddened Carlos to see it in such disrepair, but what could one old man do?

He caught up with Jaci just as she stepped into the courtyard.

"Why is it the swimming pool has been left in such a state of disrepair?" she asked. "It's seems a shame not to use it when the setting is so enticing."

"With all the gulf to swim in, why would one need a cement pool?"

"Yet someone built it here."

Yes, and if it were up to Carlos, he'd have had the hole filled in so that there was no sign it had ever existed. The *señora* wouldn't hear of it.

"What kind of fish do you catch around here?" Jaci asked.

Thankfully, she'd let the subject of the pool drop. "Flounder, redfish, pompano— too many to name."

"I'd love to try my hand at catching some of them. Would you consider taking me out in your boat? I'd pay you, of course."

He knew it was a mistake to leave his boat out in the open for renters to see. They always thought it should be at their disposal, the way they thought he should be. "I'm having a little trouble with my motor right now. If I get it fixed, I'll let you know."

He didn't know why he'd said that, but maybe taking her fishing wasn't such a bad idea. It would give him a chance to check her out, see if she was just a tourist as she claimed, or another of the curious here to search for answers to the Santiago mystery, or go ghost hunting.

He waited for Jaci to enter the gate, then headed to the main house to search for the *señora*. He saw her standing at the window, staring down at him. The look on her face was anything but pleasant. And this was even before he told her of Raoul's visit.

"I DON'T WANT HIM HERE," she said, speaking in Spanish though she spoke fluent English. She'd learned it as a young girl and now mixed the two languages as if they were one.

This was exactly the reaction Carlos had expected. He dropped into one of the uncomfortable antique chairs in Alma's sitting room and prepared himself for a bout of her childlike pouting.

"He's my brother's grandson," he countered.

"He doesn't like me."

Carlos couldn't argue that with her. Raoul had no more use for her than Emilio had had. "You don't have to see him. He'll stay in the boathouse with me if he spends the night. Most likely he won't stay that long."

"What does he want?"

"He didn't say. I assume he only wants to see me and assure himself that I'm doing well."

"Of course you're doing well. Why wouldn't you be?"

"Maybe because I'm getting older, even older than his own grandfather was when he died."

Her expression changed from one of

pouting irritation to apprehension. "Don't talk like that, Carlos."

He placed his rough hands on her thin shoulders. "Relax, *señora.* I'm not planning to die anytime soon. Raoul will visit and then he'll leave. Nothing will change."

She exhaled slowly and the drawn lines of her face eased. For a second, he caught a glimpse of the beautiful, sensual woman who used to live behind her dark, tortured eyes. Then she'd reminded him so much of another woman. But she'd never had her grace, her sweetness or her courage.

He stepped away, and the *señora* walked back to the window where she spent so much time.

"What were you talking about with the new tenant?" she asked without turning her gaze from the island and the gulf beyond.

"Fish."

"What about them?"

"She wants to pay me to take her fishing."

"I don't trust her."

"You don't trust anyone who comes to Diablo except Enrique."

"They shouldn't be here. Andres would never have let strangers roam his island."

"Things are different now, and Cochburn is within his legal rights to take in tenants." Andres's will had stated that if anything happened to him, Alma Garcia and Carlos could live on the island rent free for the rest of their lives.

It was a generous provision, the trust set up with a close attorney friend who'd let the *señora* and Carlos live on the island without the bother of tourists. But he had retired, and his son who took over the business had no allegiance to Andres.

Renting to tourists had been his idea, but when it failed to bring in the dollars he'd hoped for, he'd let the villa and the island fall even further into ruin.

"Are you on Cochburn's side now?" Alma demanded.

"I'm not on anyone's side. I just don't see the point of worrying over every tenant who comes to the island."

"How can you say that after the disasters we've had? Undercover cops. Women on the run. Investigative reporters."

"Jaci appears to be harmless."

"She was out on the beach last night after midnight, Carlos. I saw her."

"It was a nice night."

"I want her off the island. Either you take care of it or I will."

He grasped the *señora*'s left hand, then tilted her chin with his other thumb so that she had to look into his eyes. "I'll handle Jaci if she needs handling. You must leave this to me. Do you understand?"

"Then get rid of her. Get rid of Raoul, too."

"Soon enough. For now, you should take it easy and stay out of the sun."

"Andres doesn't want strangers on his island."

Carlos shoved his hands into his pockets and backed from the room. His promise to take care of things was empty. The thing that needed the most care was the *señora,* and he had no idea how to reach a woman who'd kept breathing but stopped living thirty years ago.

JACI STARED OUT THE WINDOW into the growing darkness. She'd dined on crabmeat omelet and toast at seven, and she was still feeling stuffed. She'd work another hour or two, then take a long walk in the moonlight before turning in.

Pulling her feet into the overstuffed chair, she rummaged through the stack of old newspaper reports until she found the article on the accidental drowning of Andres Santiago's only son. The boy had been four years old, but reportedly a good swimmer.

The investigation had been less than what would be routinely expected in a drowning of that sort. Two cops had come over from Everglades City. They'd questioned the child's stepmother, Medina Santiago, and apparently bought her story that the boy, who was just getting over measles had been weaker than usual and must have passed out while swimming in the deep end of the pool.

A notation at the end of the report said that the nanny, Alma Garcia, had discovered the body, and that Andres Santiago had not been home at the time of the drowning.

Jaci was certain the investigating cops would have known Santiago was a powerful drug smuggler, one who outsmarted them at every turn. They'd never been able to curtail his operations, much less stop them. Was that why they'd exerted so little energy on investigating the son's drowning, or the later disappearance of the rest of the family?

Leaving her notes, Jaci crossed the room and grabbed her navy jacket from the back of a wicker chair where she'd left it. The wind always seemed to pick up when the sun went down. She started toward the pool, but stopped when she caught sight of Alma slipping through the courtyard gate in a flowing white dress.

Jaci hurried to the gate and followed at a distance. The woman's bare feet seemed almost to float across the sand, and her skirt caught the wind, billowing about her legs. She didn't stop until she reached the water's edge.

Jaci thought at first she was going to walk right into the surf, but instead she began to twirl like a ballerina, gliding over the sand, laughing as if she were listening to a private and very humorous conversation.

Jaci continued to watch, hypnotized by the graceful movements and the silver streaks of moonlight that illuminated the lone figure. Watching Alma now, it was difficult to believe she was the same white-haired woman who stared from the third-floor window.

The twirling stopped as suddenly as it began, and Alma stood very still, her arms open as if she were waiting for a lover to step into them. Perhaps this was some kind of ritual, Jaci decided, or maybe Alma Garcia had experienced the isolation of Cape Diablo for too many years.

And then the lover arrived, albeit invisible. When Alma began to dance again, it was a waltz, and it was clear she was dancing with an imaginary partner.

The mesmerizing scene was sweetly romantic, yet somehow disturbing at the same time. In fact, Jaci had the uneasy feeling that someone was watching her watching Alma.

She scanned the beach, but didn't see any sign of Carlos, and the three of them were the only people on the island.

She turned away from Alma and walked back to the courtyard. Her mind still on the older woman and her bizarre dance, Jaci walked to the edge of the pool and stared into the murky water.

It hit her again how strange it was that the nanny, who'd once found the body of a boy she was paid to tend floating in this very pool, still lived here. In the same house where the Santiago daughters who'd been in her care had lived before the bloody night they'd disappeared with their parents, never to be heard from again.

Jaci shivered. And then she saw a new shadow mingling with hers, one that she was certain did not belong to Carlos or Alma Garcia.

Chapter Three

Startled, Jaci stared accusingly at the man who'd appeared from nowhere. "Who are you?"

"Sorry if I frightened you. My name's Raoul, and you must be Jaci."

"How do you know that?"

"Took a wild guess."

"That's not funny."

"Carlos said there was a woman named Jaci staying in one of the pool house apartments. He failed to warn me you were territorial."

Okay, so she'd come on a little strong. Still... "You could have let me know you'd walked up behind me."

"I wasn't exactly tiptoeing around. You were just so fascinated by whatever you were staring at, you didn't hear me. Besides, the courtyard is a common area, or at least it used to be."

"It still is," she said, feeling unjustly chastened. "But I thought I was the only tenant on the island."

"Technically, you are. I'm here visiting my uncle—Carlos."

For some reason, she'd assumed Carlos Lazario had no relatives, probably because none had ever been mentioned in the police or newspaper reports. Which was why a good criminologist could never trust assumptions.

"So now that I've established I'm not a pirate from the high seas here to rape and plunder, why don't we start over?" The stranger stepped closer and extended his right hand. "Pleased to meet you, Jaci."

She shook it, more amiable now that she knew he was Carlos's nephew. Maybe befriending Raoul would be the way into the old man's heart, or more specifically, into his boathouse and villa.

It was hard to tell much about Raoul's features in the dim courtyard lighting, but she did note a slight resemblance to Carlos. Something about the mouth and the shape of the eyes, she thought. But Raoul was much younger, thirty something, she'd guess. And way sexier.

"It's a nice night," he said, "cooler than this afternoon."

"Very nice. Do you visit Cape Diablo often?"

"I try to check on Carlos when I can."

"I'm sure he's glad for the company. He must get lonely out here."

"You'll never get him to admit that."

"Guess he likes isolation."

"That and he's incredibly hardheaded, just like my grandfather. Actually, Carlos is my great-uncle. He and my grandfather were brothers."

"I suppose the hardheaded trait missed you," Jaci said, finally managing a smile.

"You got it. I'm a rational, thinking man, and I'll butt heads with anyone who says differently." Raoul propped a foot on the rim of a clay flower pot full of blooming verbenas, and looked into the murky water. "I hope your room's in better shape than the pool."

"It's clean, and the bed is comfortable."

"This pool is disgusting."

"I asked your uncle about it. Apparently it hasn't been used in a very long time."

"Try three decades. It should have been filled in years ago."

"Or at least drained and cleaned," she agreed. "Is there a reason why it's been left like this?"

"Not that I'm aware of, but it's a waste of time wondering how or why my uncle and Alma Garcia do anything on Cape Diablo. I gave up years ago."

So he'd been coming to the island for a long time, maybe all his life. He might have even known the Santiago children, though he'd have been so young, Jaci doubted he'd remember much about them.

Raoul stooped to fish a plastic cup from the algae-filled pool. Jaci took the opportunity to study him more closely.

He was lean and fit, as if he worked out or engaged in physical activity on a regular basis. Dressed in denim cutoffs and a short-sleeved knit shirt open at the neck, even though she found the night wind cool. Dark hair. Probably dark eyes as well, though she couldn't tell in this light.

Not classically handsome, but with a rugged sexual appeal that seemed to stem as much from his self-confident manner as his looks.

"So what brings you to Cape Diablo?" he asked, once he'd tossed the cup in a nearby trash basket.

"I needed some downtime, and a secluded island seemed the perfect place to find it."

"That's about all you'll find here. That, snakes and every kind of annoying insect you can imagine."

She hoped to find a whole lot more, and Raoul might be just the person to help her get it. "Will you be around awhile?"

"A couple of nights, but I probably won't be here much during the day. I'm hoping to take Carlos fishing. He likes to catch the big ones, and his boat is too small to handle the waves in the open gulf."

"I didn't hear your boat come in."

"Purrs like a kitten. It's a lot quieter than the generator, except when I first start up the engines."

She dropped to the edge of one of the webbed lounge chairs, hoping Raoul would do the same. He didn't.

"The island must have a fascinating history," she said, looking up at him with what she hoped was a natural and slightly seductive smile. "Do you know much about the original builders of the villa?"

"I'm not big on history." He slapped at a mosquito that was buzzing around his neck. "Not fond of mosquitoes, either, so I think I'll head back down to the boathouse. If I don't see you again, enjoy your vacation."

So much for her feminine wiles. "Thanks."

She gave a slight wave as he retreated. But she had no intention of letting him get off that easily. She'd find a way to talk to him again.

He knew about the history of the island, but didn't want to get into it with her. Why else would he have turned and run the minute she mentioned it? It couldn't have been the mosquito. If he'd been avoiding those, he'd never have ventured out in the first place.

And even if she got nothing from him except company, it wouldn't be a total loss. The solitude might suit Carlos, but as far as Jaci was concerned, it was growing old fast.

Her mother might not be able to push her into the path of a sexy man, but isolation and an old murder case could do the trick.

RAOUL TOOK THE LONG WAY back to the boathouse, still trying to decide the best way to accomplish what he was here for, but now also thinking about Jaci Matlock. Needing downtime wasn't much of an explanation for why a young, good-looking woman would come to a secluded island by herself.

Maybe she had some big decision she was wrestling with and wanted uninterrupted time to think, or she could be getting over a man. Losing someone you loved could make a loner of you. Who knew that better than him?

Raoul slowed as he caught sight of Alma a few yards ahead of him, crouched between two clusters of sea oats. She was down on her knees, and sand was flying around her as if she were in a whirlwind.

A few steps closer, and he could see the small plastic shovel moving so fast it seemed to be gas propelled. He doubted she was building sand castles, but then who knew with Alma Garcia?

The woman was nuts. He'd first realized that when he was about ten and she'd kept calling him by the name of the Santiago kid who'd drowned in the pool. And then there was the time he'd run into her on the beach and she'd said she was looking for Pilar and

Reyna because they had run off from their lessons. That had been four years after the girls and their parents had disappeared.

As far as he could tell, Alma was getting worse all the time. The woman should be living in a home someplace where she could get medical attention, not roaming the beach alone all hours of the night. She was probably the reason Jaci had spooked so easily.

But he didn't dare mention that to Carlos again, not after the way he'd exploded the last time Raoul had suggested the woman get psychiatric help.

Raoul didn't even begin to understand the relationship between his uncle and Alma Garcia. Misguided loyalty, his grandfather had called it. Carlos thought Andres Santiago expected him to care for his children's nanny, and Carlos had never failed his old boss, even if it meant staying on Cape Diablo and looking after Alma until one of them died.

Raoul planned to make sure that didn't happen, which was why he was here.

JACI WENT TO BED AT NINE, mainly because there was nothing better to do. Yawning, she stretched between the crisp white sheets, only to have macabre images of blood splatters start creeping through her mind. Two people had been shot and killed in the boathouse, one at much closer range than the other. Two and only two, though four had disappeared. There might also have been two shooters, one taller than the other, or else the killer had changed positions or been struggling with one of the victims when the gun went off.

That was as much as she could be sure of from the photos of the splatters—or at least relatively certain. It was unfortunate that some of the blood hadn't been collected and preserved.

Not that they had any DNA from Andres or Medina to compare it with, but if the samples from the boathouse had included the blood of Andres's daughters, DNA tests would have indicated the relationship.

Jaci's mind went back to the police reports, most of which she'd memorized.

The beds of the Santiago children were unmade. The sheets, blanket and pillowcase had been stripped from one bed. Even the pillow was missing. The second bed was mussed, with the covers pulled back as if it had been slept in. The bed in the master bedroom was neatly made. There was no sign of a struggle and no blood found anywhere inside the villa.

And after that night neither the girls nor their parents were ever seen again. So the questions remained: had Andres and Medina been murdered in the boathouse upon returning from a Mexican Independence celebration? If so, what had happened to the bodies? And where were the girls, Pilar, age eight, and Reyna, age ten? Kidnapped or murdered?

So many questions without answers, and no real clues, at least none that Jaci had found yet. It would have helped if she could have gotten in touch with Mac Lowell and heard his impressions from the night he'd taken the photos.

She was still hopeful he'd show up in Everglades City, or at least get the messages she'd stuck under his door there. But even if he did, she wasn't sure how he'd get in touch with her. Her cell phone was basically useless.

A good project required more than

remarks on blood splatters and a weak hypothesis. She needed pertinent information from Carlos and Alma, something that hadn't come out before. And she needed to get inside that villa.

Giving up on sleep, she slid her legs over the side of the bed to pad to the refrigerator for a snack. She sliced into a juicy orange just as her cell phone blasted—the first call to get through since she'd arrived on the island. She sprinted across the room and grabbed it before the connection was lost.

Her hello was a little breathless.

"Is this Jaci Matlock?"

"Yes. Who is this?"

"Mac Lowell. I heard you were looking for me."

"I am."

"What do you want?"

"I understand you were part of the original investigating team the night the Santiago family disappeared."

"That was years ago."

"I know, but I really need to talk to you about the photos you took."

"Sorry, lady. You'll have to go to the Everglades City PD for anything to do with that case."

"I have been to them, and they gave me copies of your reports and the photos."

"I doubt that."

"No, they did. I'm a criminologist investigating the case." That was close to the truth. She was just a degree and a job offer away from being official.

"Then you know all I do. More, actually. I've had way too many margaritas since then to remember details."

Static crackled in her ear. She'd likely lose the connection any second. "Look, I won't take up much of your time, but I'd really like to talk to you."

"You're talking."

"The connection's already breaking up, and the chances of getting through to you again are not good. I'm staying in an apartment on Cape Diablo, but I think I can get someone to take me to Everglades City."

The pause lasted so long she feared they'd been disconnected. When Mac Lowell finally answered, his tone seemed almost fearful. "What the hell are you doing there?"

"I just wanted to see the scene of the crime for myself."

"Does Carlos Lazario know why you're there?"

"No."

"Keep it that way. And if I were you, I'd get off that island tonight. Get off and stay off."

"Why? Is Carlos dangerous? Was he involved in the crime?"

"I didn't say that."

"Ten minutes of your time. That's all I'm asking."

The phone crackled like crazy, causing her to miss half of what he said next.

"Did you say Slinky's Bar?" she asked, trying to verify what she thought he'd said.

"Tomorrow at two. Take a seat at the back of the bar and don't tell anyone why you're there."

"How will I find Slinky's Bar?"

The connection splintered or else Mac Lowell broke it. He obviously didn't want to talk to her. He might not even show, but she'd find Slinky's Bar and be waiting at two.

Grabbing a pen, she checked her caller ID for the number he'd phoned from, then scribbled it on a pad of paper, along with his name and Slinky's Bar at two.

It wasn't until she'd picked up her orange and taken a big bite that Mac's warning started echoing in her head. He seemed to believe that staying on the island put her at risk. But from whom?

Surely not Carlos. He couldn't go around murdering tenants like a character in a grade B horror movie. Someone would have noticed long before now. And not Alma. She was strange, but much too frail and pathetic to be a real threat.

Still, Jaci checked the locks on the door before she crawled back into bed. This time when she slid beneath the covers, she fell into a troubled sleep where nightmarish bodies entwined with the roots of mangrove trees.

And Raoul Lazario swam naked in a murky pool.

RAOUL LEANED AGAINST THE DOCK'S end post and took a long drink from the bottle of cold beer Carlos had just handed him. A few clouds had blown over earlier, but the sky was clear now. Heaven's bejeweled curtain,

Allison used to call it when the sky sparkled with stars the way it did tonight.

"You brought in any interesting treasures lately?"

Raoul pulled his thoughts from the past and turned to Carlos. "We uncovered a couple of ancient Greek statues on a ship in the Aegean Sea. I'm not exactly sure of their historic or archeological significance, but the man who financed the dive was excited."

"Ancient Greek statues. It must have been an old ship."

"Sank in the sixteen hundreds." Old ships had always held more interest for Raoul than their cargo. Not that anything held much interest for him these days.

He watched a stingray as it swam out from beneath the dock. "I'm thinking of taking a couple of years off."

"To do what?" Carlos asked.

"I don't know, just something besides dive for lost treasure."

Tamale joined them, carrying a worn tennis ball that he dropped next to Carlos. It started to roll, but Carlos grabbed it before it reached the edge of the dock. He picked it up and threw it without saying a word to the dog.

"It wasn't your fault, you know."

Funny. Raoul hadn't mentioned Allison once since he'd arrived on the island, but he knew that was what Carlos was talking about now, the same way Carlos knew it was why he'd lost his zeal for diving.

Carlos was insightful. He was also wrong. "It *was* my fault."

"I don't see how you figure that."

"I'd rather not get into that tonight."

Carlos reached down to wrestle the ball from Tamale and toss it again. "You remind me a lot of Emilio. You're smarter than either of us, but as stubborn as the rest of the Lazarios."

"Grandpa was smart. You are, too."

"We never did much with it. Not like you. You went out there and made a name for yourself. You even got a movie made about you."

"The movie never mentioned me."

"But you inspired it. You brought up that ship off the coast of Argentina and recovered a wealth of Spanish history with it. Emilio was so proud when the movie came out, he couldn't quit talking about it long enough to drink a beer with me. Guy let two Coronas get plumb hot."

"That doesn't sound like Grandpa."

Carlos chuckled. "We had some good times, Emilio and me. Guess we could have had more, but I was stuck out here on Cape Diablo, and he didn't like coming out here."

Now they were getting somewhere. "Why did you stay all those years?"

"It seemed the right thing to do."

"Does it still seem right?"

"We need another beer," Carlos said, avoiding the question.

"I'll get it."

"No, you stay put," he insisted. "I've got to take a bathroom break, anyway. Bladder don't work any better than the rest of me these days."

Tamale jumped back on the deck as Carlos headed toward the house. Only this time it wasn't the ball that was clutched in his teeth.

"What you got there, boy?" Raoul clicked his tongue against the roof of his mouth a few times and Tamale crept over with his tail tucked between his legs, as if he thought he might be in trouble for returning without the ball.

"It's all right, boy. I just want to see what you found."

Tamale dropped the object at Raoul's feet. He stooped and retrieved it. A bone. Human. Much too small to have belonged to an adult.

And suddenly Raoul was taken back to when he was a kid and dropped into the scariest night of his life.

Chapter Four

Carlos and Emilio were sitting on the dock having a beer. Raoul had been playing in the sand, making a fort, with twigs for toy soldiers. He'd gone inside to go to the bathroom, and he guessed they hadn't heard him come back out.

If they had known he was around, his grandfather would have never repeated the horrible things he'd told Carlos about what he thought had happened to Pilar and Reyna.

Raoul had been only six at the time, but his grandfather's words had frightened him so badly that he'd spent the entire night hiding under Carlos's bed. If something so terrible could happen to Pilar and Reyna, then it could happen to anyone on the island—even him.

He hadn't returned to Cape Diablo until he

was eleven. Even then he hadn't ventured far from his grandfather's side.

"What you got there?" Carlos asked now as he ambled back toward the dock.

Raoul pushed the memories to the back of his mind. "Looks like a leg bone."

"Probably driftwood. Let me see it."

Carlos's hand shook as he exchanged the beer he'd brought Raoul for the bone. The tremors were new, a reminder of how important it was that Raoul succeed in his mission.

"It's a bone," Raoul assured him, "and human. I've scavenged enough sunken ships to know one when I see it."

"Guess you're right," Carlos said, turning the object over so that he could see it from every angle. "Never know what will wash up out here." He tossed the bone into the waves before Raoul could stop him.

Raoul decided thirty years was long enough to avoid a subject. "I'm surprised no one ever found the bodies of the Santiago family."

Carlos stuffed his hands into his pockets and stared out at the water, though there was not much to see in the dark. "No one's ever proved they're dead."

"Or that they're alive."

"Right," Carlos agreed, "so any theory on what happened to them is just groundless speculation."

"But you must have one. Do you think Andres staged his family's disappearance?"

Carlos slapped at a mosquito, stepping backward as he did, and almost tripping over Tamale, who was crouched at his heels. "Guess a man might do anything if he had reason enough."

"You and Andres Santiago must have been close."

Carlos nodded. "He saved my life once. That binds men."

"How did that happen?"

"It was back when I served with General Norberto. Andres had come to our camp to deliver some guns and ammunition he'd smuggled into the country. A bunch of guerillas jumped us and one got a fix on me. Andres took him out before he could kill me."

A gust of wind caught wisps of Carlos's thinning, gray hair and blew it into his face. He raked it away, then looked straight at Raoul. "All that's past. No use in bringing any of it up now."

His tone made it clear the topic was closed. The adage that elderly men spent more time in the past than the present didn't hold true with Carlos. Or if it did, he didn't want to talk of it with Raoul.

"It's getting late," Carlos said, "past my bedtime."

And not nearly Raoul's. Sleep avoided him most nights until the wee hours, so he avoided laying his head on the pillow until his eyelids were so heavy they'd close without a fight.

"You turn in when you're ready," Raoul said. "I'll sleep on the boat."

"No need. You can take my bed. I'll stay in one of the guest rooms in the main house. We only have the one renter and she's in the pool house."

Even if there had been a dozen renters, there would be room in the big house. "I'm surprised you never moved up there permanently. Surely it's more comfortable than the boathouse. Definitely more roomy."

"I've thought about it, but I like my own space. The boathouse suits me. It's clean and private. Mostly, it's home."

"More reason I shouldn't run you out of it," Raoul said.

"You're not. I'm offering. A man gets pleasure from sharing his house with kin, and you're the only family I got left."

"In that case, I'll stay in the boathouse."

"You plan to do some fishing tomorrow?" Carlos asked.

"I'd like to. I was hoping you'd go with me. We can take my boat and hit the open gulf."

"That would be good, just like old times, 'cept we got that lady staying here—that renter I told you about."

"I met her when I took a walk up to the courtyard. She seems capable of taking care of herself for a day."

"It's not that, it's just…" Carlos rubbed his whiskered chin with the back of his hand. "The guests are on their own, but still I hate to leave a woman who's not familiar with the place out here by herself."

"Alma would be here."

"Yeah."

His answer was evasive, but his expression was troubled. Evidently he realized Alma would be no help to Jaci or anyone else, no matter what the emergency.

"Get some sleep," Raoul said, not wanting

talk about Alma tonight. "We can see about fishing tomorrow."

Carlos nodded. "There's food in the boathouse if you want a midnight snack. Cereal and stuff like that. Plenty of cold beer, and a bottle of whiskey on the shelf over the sink."

"I'll be fine."

"Then I'll just get a few things and head to the villa." Carlos took the path to the boathouse, Tamale at his heels. He stopped after a few steps and turned back to Raoul. "How would you feel about taking another fisherman along—or in this case, a fisherwoman?"

Raoul balked. No way was he buying into that. "I don't think Alma—"

"Not Alma. Jaci asked me to take her fishing, but I'm sure she'd have a lot more fun on a boat like yours. Besides, my motor's acting up."

Raoul mulled over the request. He'd hoped for some quality time when he'd have Carlos's full attention and no interruptions. Jaci's presence would make that impossible.

His great-uncle took off his hat and ran his hands through his thinning hair. "There's nothing wrong with going fishing with a good-looking female."

"That's not the issue."

"Isn't it? How long has it been since you've been with a woman?"

Raoul tensed. He hadn't expected anything that direct from Carlos. "I'm with women all the time. Some of my best divers are women."

"You know that's not what I meant."

He knew exactly what Carlos meant, but there was no way he was discussing his sex life with his aging uncle. "We can take Jaci along if she wants to go. It's no big deal."

"Good. I'll check with her in the morning," Carlos said, yawning through the last of the sentence.

Raoul watched him walk away. Unfortunately, the question Carlos had asked didn't recede with the man and his dog. The truth was Raoul hadn't been with a woman in any kind of romantic or intimate way since Allison.

Two years plus. Twenty-seven months of aching loneliness.

Twenty-seven months of guilt.

He didn't expect a day with Jaci to change any of that. Yet she was on his mind now, and he wondered again what had bought her to Cape Diablo's isolated shores.

JACI HAD SLEPT UNTIL NEARLY 9:00 a.m., the latest she'd stayed in bed since the fall semester had started. Normally she would have been up by seven, but she'd lain awake for hours, tossing and turning and staring out the window into the darkest night imaginable.

She blamed her inability to sleep on the unfamiliar cacophony of sounds. The drone of the generator. The roar of waves crashing on the island's western shore. The hooting of an owl. The chorus of a thousand tree frogs.

But it wasn't just the noise. It was an apprehension she couldn't explain, the feeling that something bad was going to happen before she got off this island.

She'd expected the place to be a catalyst for the investigation, but she hadn't expected the aura of mystery to be so intense.

The isolation had a lot to do with that, but the island's inhabitants certainly added to the eerie ambiance. Carlos Lazario and Alma Garcia were the strangest of bedfellows. Carlos was weathered but sturdy, like the mangroves that endured whatever storm come their way. Alma was more like the thin sea oats that swayed in the slightest breeze.

Yet they both seemed to belong to Cape

Diablo, just as the crumbling villa did. Jaci stared at the vines that crept up the white stucco walls and twined around the second-floor loggia. The few remaining bougainvillea blossoms had turned brown, but she could well imagine them in full bloom, a riot of scarlet.

Wilma St. Clair's painting didn't seem nearly as bizarre now that Jaci had arrived on Cape Diablo. Fingers of blood gripping the walls fit the sinister feel of the place much better than colorful blooms.

Jaci padded to the kitchen and took a bowl from the cabinet over the sink. She'd have a bit of cereal, then get down to her real business of the day—finding transportation to Everglades City to meet with Mac Lowell before he changed his mind.

JACI TOOK A DIFFERENT PATH to the boathouse, one that skirted the eastern coastline of the island and wound through the mangroves instead of along the sandy beach. Birds chattered and shrieked in the trees, as if scolding her for invading their territory. Dragonflies and wasps flitted among the brush, and she stopped more than once to swat away a mosquito or wipe sticky spiderwebs from her face and hair.

The area wasn't as frightening as the swamp would have been, but still it left her more uncomfortable than she would have expected.

She was almost to the clearing when she caught a whiff of cigar smoke. She had to search for the smoker. Finally, she spotted him standing under a tree a couple of yards away. He showed no sign of having noticed her, so she stepped off the path and behind a thick growth of palmetto to check him out.

Hispanic male, probably six-two, late fifties, lean but muscular, tattoos on both arms that looked to be dragons of some kind. No obvious weapon.

She left her cover and stepped back to the path. When he noticed her, she gave a wave.

"Good morning," he said, tipping a Miami Dolphins cap. He seemed friendly and normal enough.

"Same to you. Are you a new tenant?"

"No. I'm a friend of Carlos and Alma, just here for a day or two."

Who'd have guessed they socialized?

The man dropped the cigar and ground it out with the toe of his boot. "Enrique

Lopez," he said, walking toward her. "I'm sure we've never met. I would remember a woman as beautiful as you."

"I'm Jaci," she said, "a tenant."

"A pleasure to meet you." He took her hand and held it for a few seconds before kissing her fingertips.

The guy's lines probably worked as often as not. He wasn't bad looking for a middle-aged man. He had that pirate thing going on with the whiskered chin and dark, unruly hair.

"Are you going somewhere in particular, Jaci, or are you just out for a morning walk?"

"I'm on my way to the boathouse to find Carlos."

"I just left there, and there was no sign of him."

"He may be at the villa," she said.

"I hope he is. That way I can surprise both him and Alma at once."

"They don't know you're here?"

"Not yet. I got in late so I slept on my boat last night. It's docked on the southern end of the island, in the deepwater cove."

"Why didn't you use the dock?"

"It is a very large yacht."

"How did you meet Alma and Carlos?" she asked, still trying to picture the strange couple socializing.

"I had engine trouble on my yacht a few years back. I docked, Carlos fixed it for me, and we hit it off. Now this has become my haven."

Cape Diablo as a haven. Jaci tried but couldn't get that image to gel. "I guess I'll see you around," she said.

"I certainly hope so."

Leaving him behind, she hurried down the path, not slowing until she stepped into the clearing near the dock. A dozen seagulls took flight, but it was the boat the birds flew over that claimed her attention.

It was an impressive vessel, at least forty feet long with the name *Quest* painted in gleaming black letters across its clean white side. The deck was wide, with a chrome railing, and the cabin was low and sleek.

If Enrique's boat was parked at the other end of the island, than this must be Raoul's—unless there was yet another guest she hadn't met. At this point, that wouldn't surprise her.

Jaci looked around. There was no sign of

Raoul or Carlos or even Tamale. Still, she took the steep steps to the boathouse. No wonder Carlos stayed in shape if he climbed these a few times a day.

The screen door was shut, but the wooden one was ajar. She listened for a second before knocking. There were no sounds of activity or conversation, but the inviting scent of fresh perked coffee was strong.

"Carlos?" She called his name softly, and when there was no answer, called again, louder this time. "Carlos, it's Jaci."

No answer, and suddenly she was keenly aware that just beyond the open door was the area that had been the primary focus of the inept investigation. This would be the perfect opportunity to have a look at it—unless Carlos walked in on her.

A second later, she pushed through the door and into the room that had once been splattered with blood. She took in everything at once, noting obvious details and the far more subtle things she'd been trained to search for.

The only way into the boathouse was through the door she'd just entered. There were windows on all sides, but they were too

far off the ground for entry unless someone
had used a ladder.

The floor was stained linoleum, worn
thin and faded from years of tracked sand
and scrubbings that had probably removed
all traces of blood. The walls were the
color of weak tea except where sun rays
coming through the window had faded
them to a yellowed white. There was no
sign of blood.

The meager furniture was old and worn,
and stacks of newspapers and old magazines
littered half the rectangular wooden table
that dominated the kitchen area. Clean but
mismatched dishes sat drying in a plastic
rack next to the stained sink.

Jaci stood in the middle of the room and
tried to picture the way it had looked the
night Alma and Carlos had walked into the
bloody scene. What had gone through their
minds? Had they been afraid? Shocked?
Angered?

Or had they just wondered, as Jaci was
now, if the infamous drug runner, his beautiful wife and his two daughters by his first
wife had been murdered in that room? And
if the Santiagos weren't killed, then whose

blood had run like a river in the boathouse that night?

Crossing the room, Jaci opened one of the two closed doors, half expecting skeletons to rattle and fall at her feet. But the door only led to the bathroom.

The second door led to a closet. She pushed aside the few pieces of clothing on hangers and stooped to get a better look into the back corners.

A couple of huge cockroaches scurried out, one crawling over her shoe in its haste to escape. Jaci jumped so fast she banged her elbow against the doorknob and yelped in pain.

"What the hell are you doing?"

She spun around to find Raoul standing in the doorway. He was barefoot and shirtless, wearing only a pair of jeans. His hair was wet, as if he'd just stepped from the shower. If he had, he had used the one on his boat and not the one in his uncle's bathroom.

"I was looking for Carlos," she mumbled.

"And you thought he was hiding in the closet?"

"Of course not," she muttered, stalling to

come up with something Raoul would buy. "I heard scratching noises and came in here to investigate. Guess it was just a mouse."

"Really? 'Cause it smells and sounds like a rat."

"It could have been," she said, choosing to ignore his grating sarcasm. "I didn't get a look at it. Anyway, when you see Carlos, will you tell him I was looking for him?"

Raoul grabbed her arm as she tried to squeeze past. "Nice try, but try again. Why were you snooping around in here?"

"I wasn't snooping, and you surely don't think I was trying to steal something."

"Not a lot here to steal," he admitted.

His fingers were still wrapped around her arm, and though there was no pressure, she was far too cognizant of his hold on her. Aware of the fresh scent of his just-washed skin and the drops of water that glistened in the hairs on his bronzed chest.

The responsiveness irritated her and sharpened her tongue. "No one told me the boathouse was off-limits, or even that Carlos actually lived here. I thought it was part of the island resort, a place to pick up fishing gear. Now get your hand off me," she demanded, "before I file a complaint with the Florida Tourism Commission."

"Ooo, now you're scaring me. Want to call in the game warden, too?"

"If it takes that."

Tamale's barking interrupted theirs. Jaci and Raoul both turned as Carlos and his dog reached the top of the steps. Raoul released her arm but didn't back off.

"What's going on here?" Carlos said. "You two arguing about something?"

"No, we were just having a conversation," Raoul said. "Jaci's here to see you." He brushed past her and grabbed a shirt from the corner post of the unmade bed.

Jaci had no idea why he'd lied, but she certainly wasn't going to volunteer the fact that she'd been digging through Carlos's things. She breathed a small sigh of relief as she walked over to stand near the table.

Carlos rested his hands on the back of a kitchen chair. "We must have just missed each other. I was up at the pool house looking for you."

"Then you go first," she said, meeting Carlos's gaze and avoiding Raoul's steely stare. "Why were you looking for me?"

"You said you'd like to go fishing sometime."

"Yes, but that can wait until you don't have company."

"But the thing is, Raoul wants to go fishing, too. We're going out today. You're welcome to join us."

She seriously doubted that Raoul shared his sentiment. That alone would have made her tag along if she hadn't had more important matters to pursue. "I'd love to go fishing with the two of you, but something's come up and I need to make a trip to Everglades City."

"Not much there," Carlos said, "unless you plan to take one of those airboat trips into the Everglades."

"No, but this is somewhat of an emergency. I have a two o'clock appointment that I have to keep. I was hoping I could hire you to take me there, but since you're busy, I'll need to charter a ferry service."

Carlos scratched his chin. "Kind of short notice to charter a boat out here."

"I realize that, but it's very important that I keep this appointment."

"I'll see what I can do," Carlos said. "I

might be able to get Bull, that is, if I can get a decent phone connection."

"Or I could use your boat and take myself," she said. "I'd pay you, of course."

"I couldn't let you do that. You'd get lost for sure."

Raoul walked over, poured himself a mug of coffee, then leaned his backside against the counter. "Kind of odd that you'd have to rush off to an important meeting, since you're on a vacation to get away from it all."

"That's the thing about emergencies," she said flippantly. "They don't ask for an itinerary before they hit."

"You're right," Raoul agreed. "So why don't I take you to Everglades City?"

"You're going fishing."

"We can do that tomorrow, barring any unforeseen emergencies. Would that work for you, Uncle Carlos?"

"Works great. Unless the wind kicks up."

Raoul's offer caught her off guard. She'd love to tell him no thanks, but the meeting with Mac Lowell was too important. "I hate to mess up the fishing trip," she said, "but I appreciate the offer. I'll be glad to pay the going rate."

"I wouldn't know the going rate, but you can buy me a drink in town."

"I can handle that. What time should we leave?"

"One-thirty should do it."

"Can we make it one? I wouldn't mind being early."

"Whatever you say, Miss Matlock."

She wasn't sure what he was up to, but if he thought she was going to tell him her reason for snooping in his uncle's closet, he had another think coming.

She wasn't the type of woman who could be intimidated by a tall, sexy man with a nifty little cabin cruiser.

Forensics was not a science for the weak.

JACI WALKED BACK TO HER apartment, grabbed a pencil and pad, then settled on one of the lounge chairs in the courtyard to make a list of questions she wanted to ask Mac Lovell.

Mostly she wanted to listen to what he had to say, but since he was the first person she'd been able to talk to who actually took part in the investigation, she didn't want to let anything slide.

Her first heading was "crime scene." Question number one—"What were your first impressions when walking into the boathouse?" His response wouldn't be as valuable now as it would have been when the experience was fresh in his mind, but it would still be helpful. First impressions of a crime scene always were.

Impressions were most important when they were at odds with the facts or the testimony of witnesses, and in this case, there were no witnesses. No servants around, though the family had employed almost a dozen. No nanny, no Carlos Lazario. They had all been away, most in Everglades City celebrating Mexico's Independence Day.

The celebration was one of the biggest in the islands—a fiesta with fireworks and dancing and, of course, lots of food and tequila.

It struck Jaci that there had been no mention in the police reports that either Carlos or Alma had been drinking. Not likely that Carlos was, since he'd had to find the way through the dark channels back to the island.

So had he remained sober just so he and Alma could come back to the island that night? And why had they come back, when the police report made it clear that none of the other servants were expected to return until the following day?

Jaci raised her gaze to the window on the third floor of the villa. Sure enough, Alma was there, staring down at the courtyard. After thirty plus years, she must know every inch of the island, yet still she stared. Jaci lifted her hand and waved. If Alma noticed the greeting, she ignored it.

Jaci worked another half hour on the notes before lack of sleep and the heat of the mid-morning sun took its toll on her concentration. Dropping her pen and pad to the tiled courtyard floor, she rose and stretched, then decided she'd think better if she got the blood moving back to her brain. Nothing like a brisk walk for that.

She went inside and put her pad on the desk, right next to her sticky note about her appointment with Mac. After a quick bathroom stop, she grabbed a bottle of water from the fridge and hurried out the door.

An hour later, hot and sweaty, she went back to the apartment for a quick shower before her trip to Everglades City. Jaci fitted her key into the lock and pushed the door open.

She took one step inside, then stopped, instantly wary. Something wasn't right. And then she saw the evidence. Someone had been in her apartment while she was walking—or else was still in there.

Chapter Five

"Who's here?"

No one answered Jaci's call, but still she
was apprehensive as she took a few steps into
the apartment. She scanned the kitchenette to
the left of the French doors. There was no sign
of anyone, and nothing looked out of place.

The sitting room was to the right, a small
space filled with wicker chairs, a couple of
small tables and a heavy wooden bookcase
with nothing on the shelves except a collec-
tion of seashells.

The book Jaci had been reading last night
had been tossed to the wicker chair nearest
the window. She was certain—or almost certain—that she'd left it on top of the bookshelf.

The real giveaway was the research
material that she knew had been in neat

stacks on the ebony desk when she left. It was in jumbled piles.

Unfortunately, she didn't have a view of the hall or the small bedroom and bath that opened off it.

"Is there a problem, *señorita?*"

She spun around. Enrique was only a few steps behind her. Surprisingly, she was glad to see him. "Someone's been in my apartment. They may still be in there for all I know."

"I'll take a look," he said.

She followed him down the hall, scanning everything as she did. The only thing of any monetary value she had with her was her laptop, and it was still exactly as she'd left it, on the table next to her bed.

Enrique stuck his head into the bathroom. "No one in here, either. Does anything seem to be missing?"

"No," she admitted, "but someone was definitely in here while I was out. They've made a mess of the things on the desk in the sitting room."

Enrique walked back down the hall and straight to the desk. She groaned inwardly. He was a friend of Alma's and Carlos's, and she should never have called his attention to the research material.

"I'm sure it's fine," she said. "I probably just imagined someone was in here. If anything, it was probably the wind that jumbled the papers."

"Your window's closed."

"Yes, but it was open earlier this morning."

The photos of the blood splatters had been tucked inside a labeled folder when she'd left. Now they were scattered across the desk.

Enrique picked one up and studied it. "What's this?" he asked, scowling as if he were trying to figure out an ancient form of hieroglyphics.

"Just pictures."

"Some kind of Rorschach inkblot test?"

"Something like that."

"Then you must be a psychologist."

"Exactly," she said, turning away from him in case the lie showed on her face. "It's really not important." She gathered the rest of the photos, opened the top drawer of the old desk and pushed them inside. "Thanks for checking out the apartment, but everything's fine."

"Anytime. I'm always glad to help a beautiful woman in distress." He trailed his fingers down her arm as if they were lovers, or at least very good friends, and his voice had taken on a decidedly seductive tone. It was time to usher him out the door.

She tried, but he stopped at the wicker chair and picked up the book she'd been reading last night. It was a basic text on blood splattering.

"I'm fine now," she said, taking the book from him and tossing it back to the chair. "But thanks for the help."

"If you have any other needs, I'll do my best to take care of those as well." He took her hand and kissed her fingertips again.

It would have been nice if she'd felt some kind of thrill. Didn't happen, so she locked the French doors behind him and rushed to the bathroom, shedding her shirt and kicking out of her shoes as she went.

She'd have to hurry now to get to the dock by one, but there was no way she could forgo a shower. She knew she reeked.

Alma. It had to be she who'd snooped through Jaci's things while she'd been out. Alma probably had a key to all the apartments and roamed around at will.

Hopefully, she was as crazy as everyone thought, and hadn't understood or cared that all the notes on Jaci's desk dealt with the infamous, unsolved Cape Diablo mystery.

And hopefully she hadn't taken the information to Carlos and Raoul. If she had, Jaci would just confess. Even if Carlos didn't like her reasons for being here, he couldn't kick her off the island. At least she didn't think he could. She'd paid for one full month in advance.

But Raoul could and probably would refuse to take her to Everglades City as they'd planned. So much for what had started out as a promising day.

She was almost certain it had been Alma who had searched her apartment, but it would be nice to know for sure, and easy to find out. Her prints would be on the book— unless Enrique had smudged them beyond recognition. And Alma's fingerprints were on record. That's one thing that had been collected during the original Santiago investigation.

Jaci picked up the volume, careful to touch it only on the corners while she slipped it into a plastic zip bag. She'd mail it to the lab at the university today. If she sent it by courier from Everglades City, they'd get it by tomorrow.

It took only a few minutes to get the package ready to go. After that, she showered and dressed quickly, then stopped at the desk to pick up the note with Mac's information on it.

The slip of paper was missing, probably shuffled around somewhere in the mess of notes.

But their meeting was in Slinky's Bar at two, so Jaci didn't really need the note. The only other information on it had been Mac's phone number, and that would still be in her cell phone under recent calls.

She locked the French doors behind her, knowing it was a waste of time. Everyone on Cape Diablo probably had access to the keys to all the apartments. It struck her as she hurried through the arched opening to the beach just how vulnerable she was on this island.

An island that reeked of decay and evil.

Cripes! She was starting to sound like her mother. There was no such thing as a cursed plot of land. Cape Diablo was just an island, nothing more.

THE SKY WAS AN AZURE shade of blue, with only an occasional whipped cream cloud to break the splendid monotony. The wind had picked up a little since morning, but the water in the small channels was still relatively calm as she and Raoul made their way through the maze of green islands toward Everglades City.

The day was so magnificent, in fact, that Jaci had started to lose the defensive edge she'd expected to need with Raoul. He wasn't overly friendly, but he hadn't said anything to indicate he knew about all the research material in her apartment.

"Nice boat," she said, slipping out of her sneakers and stretching her legs along the curved seat that hugged the bow. "Do you spend a lot of time on it?"

"Not that much anymore."

"What a shame. It's a beautiful vessel."

He nodded.

Definitely a man of few words. She gave up on the effort to engage him in conversation, and leaned back to enjoy the scenery. A fish jumped ahead of them, its fins shining like gold in the bright sunshine.

A few minutes later, she spotted a long,

green snake stretched out on a limb hanging over the water. And on the other side of the channel, a blue heron scouted the beach, lifting each leg, then cautiously lowering it as if walking on hot coals.

A small loglike snout caught her attention. "Look! There's a baby alligator," she said, pointing to the bank where the small reptile was sunning.

"Probably a watchful mother close by then," Raoul stated.

Jaci searched the area but caught no sight of a dangerously wary parent. "It's amazing how this area thrives with life."

"And we're seeing only a small portion of it," Raoul replied, finally letting a bit of enthusiasm seep into his voice. "There's lots more beneath the surface of the water."

He steered the boat to the right, passing a sandy slope of yet another island, and a half-dozen huge turtles sleeping in the sun. "Have you ever dived?"

"Many times," she said. "My mother and her husband gave me diving lessons when I was sixteen, then took me to the Great Coral Reef off the coast of Australia to try out my new skills. From that moment on I was pretty much hooked. How about you?"

"I was hooked early, too," he admitted, "but I didn't get to Australia until much later."

She'd probably sounded like a snob, throwing out the Australian adventure like that. She hadn't meant it that way. But the experience had been so exciting.

Not that it mattered what Raoul thought of her. She'd probably never see him again after today, and she was still certain he had an ulterior motive for taking her to Everglades City. Sooner or later, he'd hit her with it. She'd prefer it be sooner so they could get it out of the way.

"Why did you volunteer to take me into town?"

"It's no big deal."

"It interfered with your fishing trip."

"I can fish tomorrow just as easily as today."

He was standing at the rudder, his unbuttoned, long-sleeved blue shirt blowing open to reveal all the details of his bronzed chest. A smattering of dark hairs started around his nipples and trailed down his flat stomach until they disappeared into the waistband of his white shorts.

She turned away quickly when he caught her staring, then adjusted her hat to block more of the sun's glare. "It's warm for late October."

"You can never tell about the weather this time of year. There are cold beers in the refrigerator inside the cabin if you're thirsty."

"Any diet sodas?"

"There should be a couple. Help yourself."

"Can I get something for you?"

"A beer would be good."

Not bothering with her shoes, she walked barefoot into the cabin. It was small but more luxurious than she'd expected—and extremely neat for a guy who traveled alone.

The living and kitchen areas were one room separated by a small bookcase. There was a brown tweed sofa, a TV, a pull-down kitchen table between two cushioned benches, and a cooking area. The bedroom and bathroom were most likely through the door behind the kitchen.

Jaci started toward the refrigerator, then stopped to examine a small framed photograph on the bookshelf. It was of Raoul standing with his arm around a strikingly beautiful woman. She had the clean-cut look of a soap model, with no apparent makeup and shiny brown hair flowing to her shoulders.

Another photo of the same woman stood beside it. This one looked as if it had been taken by a professional photographer. It was signed, "To Raoul, All my love forever, Allison."

So there was a woman in Raoul's life, though he wasn't wearing a wedding ring. Jaci's mother would be proud that she'd noticed that much.

Jaci retrieved the drinks and rejoined Raoul on the deck. This would have been the perfect opportunity to get his take on why Carlos had stayed on Cape Diablo for so many years—that is, if he hadn't already caught her snooping in the man's closet.

Raoul thanked her for the beer, but barely let her get seated again before he nailed her with a piercing stare. "Why did you really come to Cape Diablo?"

She bristled at his tone. If he thought he was going to put her on the defensive, he was wrong. "I don't owe you any explanation for why I rented the apartment."

"You people just don't give up, do you?"

"*You* people?"

"Yeah, Miss Matlock, you people who think every unsolved crime is your oyster. I know all about your little school project."

"So you're the one who broke into my apartment?"

"When did someone break into your apartment?"

"Like you don't know."

"I didn't break into your appointment."

"Then how do you know so much about my business?"

"The form you filled out when you rented the apartment asked for next of kin. You gave your mother's name."

"And you called her to spy on me?" His gall amazed Jaci.

"Considering your snooping behavior, I thought it important to know if you're a thief or just a nosy liar. Your mother wasn't home, but her housekeeper was most helpful with her explanation that you're working on a project for a graduate degree in forensic science."

"So you got me," she said, taking a huge swallow of her drink. "It's not as if I'm breaking a law. The suspicion of foul play and the few police records that exist regarding the Santiago family are public record."

"My uncle's not part of the public record, and breaking and entering was a crime the last time I checked."

"I didn't break in. The door was open, and I thought the boathouse was part of the resort, not a private residence."

"Don't take up poker, Jaci. You're a sorry liar."

"Okay, so I looked around. It's not as if I planned to hold him hostage."

"No, you were going the subtle route—talk him into taking you fishing, and worm your way into his confidence."

"Is that what you think I'm doing?"

"Isn't it?"

Actually, it was, but when Raoul said so, it sounded a lot more underhanded than what she'd planned. "You make it sound as if Carlos has something to hide."

"No, but that wouldn't keep you from trying to pin something on him."

"I'm in forensic *science*. We examine evidence, not fabricate it."

Raoul took a long swig of his beer. "Carlos

was cleared years ago. He's an old man. He's paid enough over the years. He deserves a little peace."

Jaci took a deep breath and focused on a jungle of mangroves to their right. She could see where Raoul was coming from, but he was making her out to be the bad guy. She wasn't.

"Look, Raoul, no matter what you think of me, I'm not here to cause trouble for Carlos or Alma Garcia."

"If that's the case, why don't you just pack your things and let me take you back to the mainland tonight? I'm sure you can conduct your 'little investigation' just fine from there."

She counted to ten to keep from hurling the half-empty soda can at him, finally deciding not to dignify his comment with a reply.

She had every right to be on the island. She stewed silently, and the more she thought about Raoul's reaction, the more suspicious she became of his motivation.

Could it be that the sexy, arrogant Raoul Lazario knew something about his uncle that he didn't want discovered? For a cold case, the Cape Diablo mystery was getting hotter by the day.

They made the rest of the trip in silence. Raoul was infuriating, which made it twice as irritating that every time she caught a glimpse of him, she was aware of how sexy he looked at the helm of the boat.

Amazing that a man like Enrique tried so hard to be seductive, and with Raoul it just seemed to come naturally, even when he was being a total ass. Even when she suspected he might have something to hide.

But then, that was probably the attraction. She'd always loved a challenge.

SLINKY'S BAR WAS THE TYPICAL beach hangout, right down to the rickety wooden sign that proclaimed No Shirt, No Shoes—No Problem. The building itself looked as if it had been constructed overnight, probably after a hurricane had ripped the last Slinky's Bar to shreds. The lingering odors of smoke, beer, body odor and mold hung heavy in the stale air.

Various beer advertisements dangled from the walls, and a jukebox in the corner was belting out a Jimmy Buffet song. Two bearded guys in Bermuda shorts and cotton shirts, tails out, sat at the bar talking to a waitress with breasts that threatened to slide out of a lime-green tank top at any second. Jaci guessed both men to be in their midfifties, though she couldn't be sure in the dim light.

The only other patrons were a group of what looked to be middle-aged vacationers at a table in the back, and two guys and two girls in their twenties playing pool.

Jaci was aware of the stares from the two men at the bar as she crossed the rough floor and took the table in the back right corner, hoping that neither turned out to be Mac Lowell. They looked far too zoned out for her to put a lot of stock in what they remembered from thirty years ago.

She tucked her handbag on the seat next to her and tried to look at ease, though she felt as out of place here as she did at her mother's society functions.

Not because it was a bar. Even though she wasn't much of a drinker, she'd been in her share of them during her years at the university. The awkwardness was due more to the fact that her reason for being here was seriously out of kilter with the atmosphere.

The waitress stopped in front of her. "What can I get you?"

"I'll have a margarita on the rocks, no salt."

Jaci kept her eye on the door, wishing Mac would show up, though she knew she was early. She waited until her drink was served, then glanced at the Budweiser clock over the bar. Still twenty minutes before two.

She made the mistake of making eye contact with one of the men at the bar. He picked up his drink, slid off his bar stool and ambled back to her table.

"Are you expecting someone?"

"Yes. He should be here any minute."

"Is he a big, burly, jealous husband?"

"No, just a… He's just a friend."

"In that case, feel free to join us until he shows up—or if he don't show up. You look too lonesome back here in the dark by yourself."

She'd hoped to look inconspicuous. "Thanks for the offer, but I'm fine."

"You here on vacation?"

"No. Just visiting." It was clear he wasn't just going to disappear voluntarily. "Would you excuse me?" she said, picking up her handbag and slipping the strap over her shoulder. "I need to go to the restroom."

"Gotcha. You're not looking for company."

He tipped his beer in her direction and went back to the bar. She followed the signs to the bathroom, hoping Mac would be here by the time she returned, or at least by the time she finished the margarita.

Mainly she just hoped he showed up.

RAOUL CHECKED THE SUPPLIES in the boat's refrigerator, then got another beer and walked back to stretch out on deck. It had been awhile since he'd been to Everglades City, but it never seemed to change much, and he had no desire to walk the narrow streets or peruse the beach bars or seashell shops.

He closed his eyes, and his mind sifted through a couple of unsettling thoughts about Carlos and Alma before settling on Jaci.

She was nice looking in a low-key, casual kind of way that made her far more seductive than if she'd flaunted her body in one of those bathing suits that fitted like dental floss. Great legs.

Nice hair, too, especially when the sun highlighted it with gold. But it was her eyes

that really set her apart. Dark lashes surrounded emerald-green irises that flashed
when she got riled.

But he wished he knew what she was
really after with this investigation. In thirty
years, no one had tied Carlos or Alma to the
Santiagos' disappearance. Even Raoul's
grandfather had never suggested that either
of them bore any guilt in the bizarre mystery.

And yet...

Raoul's mind drifted back years to a hot
night when he'd been sneaking to the play-
house Pilar and Reyna's father had built
them in a cluster of mangroves. Raoul
couldn't have been more that five. He didn't
have a lot of memories that went back that
far, and this one was hazy.

Fragments of the conversation came back
to him now. A body floating in the pool. An
evil witch. And plans for how they were
going to kill her. He'd run back to the boathouse when they'd started talking about
killing witches. He'd told his grandfather,
who'd said they were just trying to scare him.

Raoul let the memories slide, and finished
his beer, already bored with nothing to do.
Strolling the streets of Everglades City might

not be such a bad way to wile away an hour or two, after all. If Jaci returned before him, she'd just have to wait.

Again he wondered exactly what she had to do in town that was so important, anyway. Anyone who had information about the Santiago mystery would have leaked it long ago.

MAC WASN'T THERE BY THE time Jaci finished the margarita, even though she'd sipped slowly and made it last as long as she could. Nor had he answered his phone.

He hadn't wanted her to come to his house, but he must know that she'd at least try to catch him there if he didn't show at Slinky's.

She pushed the empty margarita glass away and glanced at the clock over the bar one last time. It was two forty-five. She paid her tab and escaped out the front door, eager to breathe air that didn't choke going down. Eager to find Mac.

Less than ten minutes later, she walked up on the porch at his house and knocked. A dog barked inside, then broke into a wail. There was no sound of footsteps or any other human noises inside the house. She knocked again. The dog wailed even louder.

Unwilling to give up, she looked around to see if Mac was outside somewhere. He wasn't, and neither was anyone else. The nearest house was half a block away, and it looked deserted.

She knocked again as she struggled with her conscience. Breaking into a house belonging to a man she'd never met before was a lot different than walking into a resort boathouse.

The dog continued to wail. She tried the doorknob. It turned and the door creaked open. The dog stood nearby, staring up at her with big brown eyes, its tail between its legs.

She knelt beside him. "What's the matter, boy? You don't look hurt. Are you hungry? Thirsty?" She stood and looked around. A nearly empty coffee cup and a saucer holding half a piece of toast set on a table near the sofa. A newspaper, opened to the sports news, was lying on the floor near a pair of green flip-flops.

"Mac?" she called, but didn't expect an

answer. The house had a quietness about it that spooked her a little.

The dog started to wail again, and Jaci hesitated only a few seconds before following him down the hall and through a doorway. Mac was there, or at least someone was.

The dog whimpered and scratched at its own face with his front paws. Jaci just stood there, staring into the room, while a cold knot of fear and icy dread settled in her chest.

Chapter Six

The body was suspended from what appeared to be a meat hook in the ceiling, the head resting at a bizarre angle that made it look as if it were unattached. The blank eyes were open, the bulbous tissue surrounding them discolored.

Jaci checked for a pulse, though she knew from the appearance of the skin and the musculature that he was dead. But he hadn't been for long. Maybe for as little as an hour. It might have happened while she was sitting at Slinky's Bar waiting for Mac to appear.

This might or might not be Mac. All she could ascertain was that the victim was a white, middle-aged or older male with a receding hairline, salt-and-pepper hair and a chunky build.

The chair kicked from beneath his feet and

lying sideways on the floor indicated it had been a suicide, or at least that someone wanted it to look like a suicide.

She took in the rest of the surroundings slowly, working through the initial shock as best she could. The dog had stopped wailing, but he was stretched out beneath the dead man's dangling feet.

The smell and feel of death consumed her as she took her camera from her purse and shot detailed photographs of the room and the body, careful not to disturb anything. Strangely, the action had a calming effect. Dissecting a crime scene was what she knew.

When she was finished, she called the local police, then walked to the porch to wait for the officers' arrival. Guilt reared its ugly head as she waited. Could her phone call to him have anything to do with Mac's death? But then, how could it?

The dog began to wail again. Maybe she was just commiserating with him, but suddenly she felt real pangs of isolation. She had never felt so alone.

RAOUL HAD ALREADY STARTED BACK toward the marina and his waiting boat when he heard the police siren. He turned to watch the squad car speed past, only to skid to a stop in front of the gaudy blue house about seventy yards down the quiet neighborhood street.

Two uniformed officers jumped from the car and strode up the walk to where a young woman was waiting. Damn. That was Jaci. Raoul didn't try to explain the swell of panic that hit as he hurried toward the house.

By the time he reached it, Jaci and the cops had disappeared through the open front door. Not one for formality, and never big on rules unless they were for other people, Raoul walked to the door and peered into the dark living room.

Seeing no one, he walked inside and followed the voices to the back of the house. The first thing he saw was the body swinging like a slab of meat in a butcher's cooler. The second was Jaci, ashen faced but toe to toe with a broad-shouldered cop who'd adopted an intimidating stance.

The other cop, younger and slim, caught sight of Raoul.

"We got company, Jake."

The burly cop turned toward Raoul as

well. "State your name and your business here."

"Raoul Lazario, and—"

"He's with me," Jaci said, walking over to stand beside him.

"You didn't say you had someone with you."

"He brought me to the island on his boat. He wasn't aware of my business dealings with Mr. Lowell."

"So neither of you admit knowing Mac?"

"Is that Mac?" Raoul asked, nodding toward the body.

"That's him," Jake said.

"Then I don't know him."

"I already explained that I found him like this when I showed up for an appointment," Jaci said, directing her frustration and her words at Jake. "I didn't even know for certain the dead man was Mac Lowell until you showed up and said it was him."

Impulsively, Raoul slipped his arm around her shoulders. Her hair brushed against him, and his insides wobbled.

A fine damn time for his libido to kick in. He let his arm slide back to his side.

"And Mr. Lazario here wasn't with you when you found the body?" Jake asked.

"No. I was alone."

"In that case I'll have to ask you to wait outside until we finish taking her statement, Mr. Lazario."

Raoul's gaze locked with Jaci's troubled one. "I'll be right outside if you need me."

"You don't have to wait. I can meet you at the boat."

"I'll wait."

"Thanks." She slipped her hand into his and squeezed.

A quick squeeze. That was it. Then she let go and turned her attention back to the cop who was asking her about the meeting she was supposed to have had with the deceased.

Raoul walked back to the porch and dropped to the top step, stretching his legs and resting his back against the support beam. He wasn't sure what had happened back there, but he knew he'd crossed some kind of line with Jaci that he'd never intended to cross.

They weren't on the same side, and he couldn't let some male protective urge lead to his messing up what he'd come to Cape Diablo to do.

Okay, so maybe the urge hadn't been strictly protective. But that was understandable considering this was the first time he'd had his arm around a woman in twenty-seven months.

Still, his loyalties lay with Carlos, even more so now that Jaci's project involved a dead man. The old crime—if there had been one—was better left buried.

Jaci would never see it that way. And Carlos could probably handle her better than Raoul was doing at this point.

The smart thing for him to do would be deliver Jaci to Cape Diablo, try to talk some sense into Carlos, then cruise into the sunset.

But Raoul had never been all that smart about pulling out when trouble stepped in.

THE LAST RAYS OF SUN WERE slashing the sky with yellow and gold by the time Jaci and Raoul made it back to the boat. She'd been silent ever since they'd left Mac Lowell's house. Her usual high level of exuberance was dulled, and even her eyes showed signs of exhaustion.

Raoul helped her onto the boat, then untied the ropes that held them to the pier. Within five minutes Everglades City faded into the grayish, green mass of islands that made up this part of the gulf.

The channels were choppier than they'd been on the trip over, but the *Quest* took them in stride.

"Your boat rides the water well," Jaci said, as if reading his mind.

"Always has. One of her strong points."

"Have you had it long?"

"About four years."

The *Quest* had been the first real luxury he'd ever owned, and he'd never have purchased it if Allison hadn't fallen in love with it.

It had belonged to a client of Raoul's, a wealthy investor who held a rabid fascination for anything that moved on water. Before Allison, all Raoul's energy and money had gone into growing his business.

They hit a wider channel with rougher water, and Jaci pulled up the hood of her jacket, tying it in place.

"You can go inside if you want," he said. "It's warmer in the cabin."

"It's not really cold, only windy. Besides, I'm hoping the salty sea breeze can clear my head of the images left over from the afternoon." She pulled her feet up on the bench.

"I wouldn't think images of death would bother someone planning a career in forensics."

"It's the science of gathering all the evidence and solving the puzzle that I like, not the dying."

"Sounds like splitting hairs to me."

"So what do you do when you're not out playing in the gulf?"

There was a time when he'd have loved fielding that question. It would have given him a chance to go on endlessly about something he'd been as passionate about as Jaci was her forensics.

"I'm a treasure diver."

"Exactly what does a treasure diver do?"

"I locate sunken ships, take my crew down and explore the remains, bringing up whatever we find of personal, anthropological or financial value. Sometimes that includes the ship."

"Sounds fascinating, especially the anthropological treasures."

"I haven't recovered all that many, but recently we salvaged some magnificent Greek statues from a ship that had sunk in the sixteen hundreds."

"Who got the statues?"

"Most are on loan to a museum in Athens. A few are in the home of a wealthy Greek art collector. He financed the exploration."

"You must get a thrill making that kind of discovery."

"I've had my moments." Good and bad, but he wasn't getting into that. "I don't know about you, but I'm hungry."

"I'm famished. I guess we should have stopped in one of the restaurants in Everglades City for food and that drink I promised you."

"You can pay up later. I have a nice cabernet and some ham and Swiss cheese for sandwiches."

"You're making my mouth water. The only thing I've had since breakfast is the soda I drank on the way over and a margarita in Slinky's Bar."

"Then ham and cheese it is."

By the time Raoul found a quiet cove to drop anchor, the sun had fully descended, and the moon was a floating silver crescent.

"We can eat on the deck or inside," he said. "If we decide on the deck, I have a small folding table I can set up."

Jaci followed him into the cabin. He opened the wine first and poured them each a glass. "Cheers," he said, clinking them together. It was the only toast he could think of that wouldn't have been awkward in their current situation.

"If we had candlelight so that we could see what we're eating, I'd prefer the deck," she said. "It has more of a spirit of adventure about it."

"I would have thought you'd had enough adventure for one day, but you're in luck. I don't think we could keep a candle burning in that breeze, but I have deck lights, nice dim ones that hopefully won't lure too many bugs."

Jaci moved out of the way while he retrieved sandwich makings from the refrigerator. The situation got to him again. Sharing space in the small kitchen seemed too familiar and intimate.

There was no explanation for the way she affected him, and that bothered him as much as anything.

"Can I do something to help?" she asked.

"How about toasting the bread?"

"I can handle that."

He shoved the loaf down the counter in her

direction. "The toaster is next to the coffee-pot."

She toasted the bread and smeared it with a spicy brown mustard while he washed and sliced a firm red tomato he'd bought at the open-air market in Naples just before he'd left for Cape Diablo.

"I'll set up the table," he said. "You're in charge of getting the food and wine outside."

"What about napkins?"

"Oops. I knew this was going too well. I'm out of napkins. Can't ever remember to put those on the shopping list."

"Good. Your preparedness level was starting to make me feel very inadequate. I'll tear off some paper towels."

Raoul caught a glimpse of the photograph of him and Allison as he carried the small table onto the deck. An instant knot formed in his throat at the poignant memory of the last time he'd shared wine and a meal with a woman on the *Quest*. That had been the night he'd asked Allison to marry him.

He swallowed past the lump. He could do this. Tonight wasn't about romance. It was about a dead man back in Everglades City, and doing right by his uncle. And about two hungry people eating a sandwich.

Neither his mind nor his body bought the lie.

THE WINE AND FOOD WORKED wonders for Jaci's frame of mind, and for some reason she didn't quite understand, Mac Lowell's death had put Raoul in a much more hospitable mood. She didn't trust it to last, but she was far more relaxed than she'd expected to be after the day's trauma.

Raoul deserved a lot of credit for salvaging at least part of the day. The rest was the ambiance—gentle waves lapping the side of the boat and a slight breeze rustling the branches of hundreds of mangroves.

She finished her sandwich, then sipped her wine, letting the fruity taste linger on her tongue as she watched the silvery thread of the moon's reflection shimmer across the still waters of the cove.

Raoul refilled both their glasses, then stretched his feet beneath the small folding table he'd placed near the bow. "Want to talk about your day?"

The offer surprised her, but the truth was

she'd like to get someone else's take on the suicide. "If I talk, will you promise not to get riled up again over my investigation of the Santiago mystery?"

"I promise not to toss you overboard."

"Good. I hate swimming with gators on a full stomach."

"I'm not happy about the investigation," he admitted in a more serious tone, "but I know you don't need my okay to do this. And I'd really like to know about your dealings with Mac Lowell."

She took another sip of wine and sifted through the troubling images. "I don't know how much you overheard, but Mac was a local policeman for a brief period of time years ago."

"Thirty years ago?"

She nodded. "He was one of the original investigators in the Santiago disappearance."

"And that's why you went to see him?"

"Yes. I had been trying to get in touch with him ever since I'd started working on the project, but I'd been unsuccessful until he called last night. Amazingly, he got through on my cell phone."

"And he agreed to today's meeting?"

"I had to talk him into it, and even then he wanted to meet me at Slinky's Bar and not at his home. I didn't understand the reasoning behind that, but I agreed."

"Then how did you end up at his house?"

She explained, and Raoul didn't interrupt until she'd finished recounting the details, including the fact that the two cops on the scene both knew Mac and both seemed shocked that he'd kill himself.

"Maybe he didn't," Raoul said. "How hard is it to stage a murder so that it looks like suicide?"

"In this particular case, it wouldn't have been difficult at all."

"My guess is he was about to squeal to you, and someone shut him up before he could."

"I knew that would be the first explanation that popped into your head."

"Didn't it pop into yours?"

"Yes, but it doesn't add up. Why would someone think he'd tell me something that he hadn't told anyone else in thirty years?"

"Maybe because he agreed to see you."

"But why would he talk now?"

"He needed to clear his conscience."

"So why would a cop keep secrets in the

first place?" she asked, realizing that she liked bouncing ideas off Raoul. Brainstorming was an excellent crime-solving tool.

"Crooked cops aren't that unusual, especially where wealthy drug runners and smugglers are involved."

"And even otherwise honest cops have been known to cooperate with criminals out of fear," Jaci added. "And Andres would have the kind of enemies who if doublecrossed wouldn't hesitate to take out a man and his whole family."

"Which is quite possibly what happened to Andres. But then you know all of that, Jaci. It's your project."

"Do you remember Andres Santiago at all?"

"If I ever met him or his wife, I don't remember them. I was not quite six the night it all went down, and the only thing I recall about the Santiagos was being frightened once by Pilar's stories about the old witch who lived in the villa."

A witch in the villa. Now that was interesting. "Do you think they could have been talking about Alma?"

"I think Pilar just liked scaring her older sister and me."

"I wonder about their stepmother," Jaci said. "From everything I read she was very beautiful, but had a fiery temper. Have you ever heard Carlos speak of her?"

"No, but then, he never talks about the past with me. It's as if he's pushed it from his memory."

"You still think my investigating the case will upset him, don't you?"

"One man is dead, Jaci. Release the secrets from thirty years ago and who's to say there won't be more victims? Who's to say the real killer isn't still nearby, watching and waiting, as desperate as ever to escape punishment? Yeah, I think this could upset him."

"If you're trying to frighten me, it won't work."

"Then you're braver than I am. I can't stop you from going ahead with the investigation, but let Carlos be, Jaci. He's got enough to deal with."

Jaci gathered their empty plates. "I think we should head back to Cape Diablo now."

"Wait." Raoul grabbed her arm to stop her from walking away. "You asked this morning if I'd broken into your apartment."

She shrugged. "You said you hadn't. I

believe you. In fact, I'm pretty sure it was Alma. She didn't take anything and may not have even realized I was staying there. Her grip on reality seems extremely slippery."

"Which doesn't mean she's totally harmless."

"Are you suggesting she might try to hurt me?"

"Probably not intentionally. Look, Jaci, I know you're not going to give up the investigation, but you don't have to stay on the island to complete your project. I think you should pack your things and let me take you back to the mainland."

"I can't do that. If the answers exist, they are on Cape Diablo."

"I could have you thrown off the island, you know."

The man was exasperating. Fuming, Jaci stamped back into the cabin and stayed there while he put the table away, pulled up the anchor and started the engine.

No way would she let Raoul order her around. Sure, she might be a little attracted to him, but so what?

She was doing just fine without a man in her life.

CARLOS WALKED OUTSIDE AND watched from the top of the boathouse steps as Raoul's cabin cruiser approached. Hopefully, the late return meant that he and Jaci had hit it off. It was past time for Raoul to jump back into life. He'd been dealt a bitter blow, but living on memories and regrets made for a painfully lonely existence. No one knew that better than Carlos.

The night air was chilly, and he reached back inside and grabbed his worn black jacket from the hook by the door. Shoving his arms through the sleeves, he took the steps a lot slower than Tamale, who was already bounding down the path that led to the deck.

Originally, the boathouse had sat right over the deck, but after losing two structures to hurricanes, Andres had rebuilt amidst a thick cluster of mangroves, leaving the bottom level open to store fishing equipment, a few tools and the kayak Carlos never used anymore.

Jaci was already out of the boat when he reached the dock. "How was the trip?" he called, letting them know he was there.

She gave him a wave. "Not quite what I expected."

That could mean anything, but something

in her voice made him doubt it was a good sign. "I've got some fish soup on the stove if you're hungry."

"Thanks, but we ate."

Just as well. He'd never invited one of the tenants to eat with him before, and it probably wasn't a good idea to start now. He wouldn't have even considered it if Raoul hadn't been there.

By the time his nephew had secured the boat and stepped onto the dock, Jaci was walking away. No goodbyes or see-you-laters. Something had passed between them, but obviously it hadn't had romantic overtones.

Then again, judging from the way Raoul was just standing there, his muscles all bunched, watching her walk off, it was pretty sure Jaci had at least gotten his attention. There might be hope for them, after all.

"Long day?" Carlos asked.

"Yeah." Raoul stooped to give Tamale a good head scratching. "I'll tell you about it inside."

Carlos suddenly felt tired and almost too weak to make it up the stairs. He stopped at the small, covered landing at the top of the steps, the one spot he could get a clear view of the beach. He glimpsed an erratic, bouncing beam of light near what the season's storms had left of the dunes. He couldn't see a figure in the darkness, but knew the *señora* was out there living the fantasy that had become her reality.

Maybe it was time someone did uncover the secrets that held Cape Diablo in this paralyzing time warp. Time for the island to be washed clean of the sinister elements that held it in a bony grasp.

But unloose the secrets and the truth might destroy them all.

JACI TOOK OFF HER SHOES when she reached the beach, and walked along the shore, wary of the jellyfish that sometimes washed onto the sand. An occasional wave lapped her feet, and she tingled from its invigorating coolness.

The beach walk was the perfect balm for her rattled nerves. Mac's death had left her edgy and confused. And Raoul totally perplexed her. He could be so darn nice one minute, a controlling ogre the next.

Worse, she had trouble controlling her

own emotions when she was with him. All she should be thinking about was how to placate him and get information from him. Instead, she'd lost her temper.

It was as if some kind of weird, combustive chemical reaction transpired when they were together.

"Pilar. Reyna."

Jaci stopped dead still as the names of the Santiago children wafted around her on a ghostly breeze.

She turned slowly, scanning the moonlit beach until she saw movement a few yards to her right. Alma, in her white flowing dress. But she wasn't dancing. She was pacing back and forth in front of the sand dunes.

If she'd noticed Jaci at all, she'd evidently chosen to ignore her. Jaci considered doing the same. She'd done enough research for one day.

"Pilar? Where are you?"

The call sent an icy finger up Jaci's spine. Alma really had lost it. Crazy, Raoul had said, but not necessarily harmless. Yet the frail, silver-haired woman in white certainly didn't look dangerous tonight.

If anything, she looked as hauntingly lost

as her voice sounded. It seemed cruel to leave her to wander the beach at night in such a tormented state.

Jaci started walking toward her. "Hi, Alma. It's me, Jaci Matlock. I'm staying in the courtyard apartment."

"What are you doing out here so late?"

The woman's voice slurred as if she'd been drinking, but there was no odor of liquor on her breath.

"I've been out on the boat today and I'm walking back to my room."

"You were on the boat with Andres, weren't you?" She sounded angry and maybe a little hurt.

"I was with Raoul."

"You lie. You were with Andres."

"No. Andres isn't here. It's getting late," Jaci said, holding out her hand. "Walk back to the house with me. We can talk about Andres on the way."

Alma pushed her hand away. "You are lying, and you have to be punished."

And that's when Jaci saw the gleam of the knife clutched in Alma's right hand, the blade pointing at Jaci's heart.

Chapter Seven

Jaci stepped back slowly. "Throw the knife down, Alma, before you hurt someone."

"Andres won't like it when I tell him what you've done." The older woman waved her hand, swinging the curved blade through the air as if it were a machete.

Jaci stood her ground, but was ready to run if it came to that. She wanted no part of a fight with an unbalanced woman wielding a knife. "Andres isn't here," she said again, working to keep her voice calm, though she was anything but.

"Don't lie to me." Alma raised the knife, than began to sway, almost imperceptibly at first, but gaining momentum until she resembled a young palm in the breeze. She moaned softly, then opened her hands, palms up, in front of her, not seeming to notice when the knife dropped from her shaking fingers.

Jaci kicked at the weapon, and it flew a few yards before burrowing into the sand. Alma pressed her temples with the tips of her fingers as if she were dizzy or in pain.

The swaying stopped, and the woman dropped her hands to her sides, her shoulders slumped as if in defeat. Jaci slipped her arms around her thin shoulders, understanding now why the poor woman spent her days staring out the window. She was searching for a sign that her young charges of so many years ago would return.

A second later Alma's body grew rigid, and she pulled away from Jaci. "You must leave Cape Diablo at once," she ordered. "You have no business here."

"Why should I leave?"

"Because…" She turned away and dropped her voice to a shaky whisper. "Because if you stay too long, Diablo will steal your soul."

Alma turned and started walking away, her loose white gown billowing in the wind. She didn't head toward the villa, but toward the boathouse.

Jaci watched until she disappeared from sight. Jaci wasn't worried that her soul would be stolen, but did wonder if Alma had lost her grip slowly, losing her mind to overwhelming guilt. Or had she witnessed something so horrifying that one bloody night that it had driven her suddenly and irreversibly mad?

The wind picked up and Jaci felt a chill clear down to her bones. But she wouldn't be seduced by the island's history or its dark atmosphere. It was long past time for Cape Diablo to give up its carefully guarded secrets.

She planned to make certain that it did.

RAOUL WAITED UNTIL CARLOS had gotten rid of Alma before straddling one of the straight-backed chairs and joining him at the kitchen table. He dreaded getting into this discussion, but it seemed only right that he level with his uncle. "I have some information you might be interested in."

Carlos looked up from the newspaper he was reading, his expression guarded. "You sound serious."

"Nothing big, but since you seem to have made friends with Jaci, I thought you might like to know what brought her to Cape Diablo."

"Don't tell me she's another one of those writers here to make up a bunch of bull about the Santiagos and call it a story."

"Not exactly." Raoul explained about her project, omitting the fact that the man she'd had an appointment with today was dead. Carlos didn't interrupt, but his occasional grunts and guffaws made his displeasure clear.

"What does she think she'll find that no one else has?"

"I don't know."

"Unless she can make evidence out of thin air and a bunch of sand, she's wasting her time."

"Right. So I wouldn't worry about her."

"She doesn't seem like a student. I took her for a grown woman."

"She's a graduate student," Raoul said, hoping to get off the subject of Jaci as quickly as possible.

Carlos wasn't ready to drop it. "Ever since they aired that stupid TV show describing the island as haunted, it seems that half the people who come are just here to find ghosts or dig into the past."

"I guess I missed that special."

"You were lucky. It was bunk."

"How did you see it?" Raoul asked. He knew there was no television on the island.

"I didn't. I just heard about it. They interviewed some crackpots who said they'd had strange experiences on the island. I'll bet you a dollar most of them had never even been here."

"I don't think the TV show has anything to do with Jaci's visit."

"But she's still here to poke around in things that are none of her business. And she had the gall to ask me to take her fishing!"

He was as mad as Raoul had ever seen him. That couldn't be good for a man in his condition. "It would be nice to know what really happened that night. At least it would give you and Alma some closure."

"I'm not looking for closure, and I'm tired of these people coming here asking me questions and upsetting the *señora*. It's our island, and they've ruined it for us. We may as well just leave and give Andres's island completely over to the drug runners."

The conversation was making Carlos more upset by the second. It probably wasn't the best time for Raoul to mention his own reasons for being here, but he wasn't likely to get a better opening than the one his uncle had just thrown out.

Raoul had given this a lot of thought, and the most straightforward approach seemed the best, and likely the only one he could pull off. He leaned in closer. "You know, Carlos, that's not such a bad idea. There comes a time when a man needs to let go of the hassles."

The older man pushed back from the table. "What are you talking about?"

"I think it's time for you to leave Cape Diablo."

His remark was met with silence and an icy stare. Not quite the reaction Raoul had hoped for, but better than having his uncle yell and order him off the island.

"You admit things aren't great here," Raoul said.

"This is my home."

"It doesn't have to be."

Carlos stiffened. "I don't know what this is about, Raoul, but don't go walking down a path you don't know."

"Sometimes a path gets too rocky for anyone to walk."

"Mine's not...yet."

"That's not the way I heard it," Raoul said, knowing he'd gone too far to turn back now.

"Then you heard wrong." Carlos stood and walked to the door to his bedroom. "I'll get my things, and then I'm going up to the villa to get some sleep. I'll be back in the morning. You can be here or not, but either way, that's the last I want to hear about my leaving Cape Diablo."

There was no putting it off any longer. It was clear Carlos wasn't going to confide in him. "I talked to Dr. Young," Raoul said. "I know about the cancer."

His uncle flinched as if he'd been hit. "He had no business calling you."

"It seems he did. I'm your next of kin."

"I gave him that information in case of emergency."

"According to Dr. Young, if you don't go in for radiation therapy, you won't see another fall. That constitutes an emergency in anyone's book."

Carlos brushed it off with a wave of his hand. "No one has any guarantees they'll see another fall."

"You have a chance with treatment. You

can stay with me in Naples. I have plenty of room. You'll have privacy, nursing care if you need it, and the doctor's office is only a five-minute cab ride away."

Carlos leaned against the door frame, the muscles in his face sagging so that for once he looked every one of his seventy-three years. "You're a good guy, Raoul. I know you want to help, but you can't. So just let it go. I'll handle this my way."

His voice fell to a gruff whisper, and when he'd finished, he ducked into the bedroom, closing the door behind him before Raoul had a chance to reply.

Raoul fought the urge to burst through the door and demand that his great-uncle listen to reason. His grandfather hadn't had a chance against the heart attack that had taken him out years too soon, but Carlos did. All he had to do was leave Alma and this snake and mosquito infested island, and seek medical care.

The fact that Carlos would give up his life to stay here with that fruitcake Alma burned in Raoul's gut like pure acid. He turned and stamped out of the boathouse, not stopping until he'd climbed onto the deck of his boat.

He stood at the helm, wishing he could

start the engines and escape back to the mainland. He stayed there until his thoughts shifted from Carlos to Jaci.

She'd been tough, had dealt with the suicide and finding Mac Lowell's body like a pro. Yet she had a softer, far more vulnerable side, too. He'd seen it in her eyes and heard it in her voice when he'd first found her in Mac Lowell's house, and then again on the boat coming back to Cape Diablo.

She was stubborn, and obsessed with Cape Diablo, so much so she'd never give up the project even if it did turn out to be dangerous for her.

But she was not his concern. That's what he had to get clear in his mind. He was here for Carlos and nothing more.

Yet he couldn't wipe her from his thoughts, and as he stood in the moonlight, he was attacked by feelings and urges that felt so out of place he had no idea what to do with them.

Finally, he went inside the cabin, undressed and climbed into bed. Sleep, as usual, was a long time in coming.

THE WATER SWIRLED AROUND RAOUL, dark and heavy, pushing him down and crushing the *walls of his chest. He needed to get back to the surface, but he couldn't, not until he located Allison. She had dived with him. She had to be here.*

And then he saw her, floating near him in the thick, blue haze, laughing and motioning for him to follow her. He swam after her, but no matter how fast he stroked, the distance between them grew greater.

His lungs were on fire now, and the water was hardening to the consistency of mashed potatoes, slowing him down even more and making his muscles ache.

He closed his eyes for a second. When he opened them, she had disappeared.

Raoul woke with a jerk, part of him still lost in the nightmare that had left him in a cold sweat. Kicking back the sheets, he raked the damp hair from his forehead with clammy hands.

He tried to swallow, but the dryness in his mouth and throat made it difficult. He dragged himself to the kitchen and filled a glass with bottled water. He gulped it down quickly, then refilled the glass, drinking slowly this time, letting the liquid soothe his parched throat.

There was never any warning that the nightmare would hit, but he hadn't expected it tonight, and certainly not so vivid. Not that the dream had been accurate. It never was. It was always a twisted version of the truth, his subconscious finding new ways to make him feel as totally useless and helpless as he'd been.

He'd thought himself invincible before that night, believed that he controlled everything he cared about. But all it took was one fatal mistake in judgment to make him realize just how human and fallible he really was.

"You didn't die that day, Raoul. Take back your life. Do it for Allison and for yourself. Life is too precious to waste."

Those had been his grandfather's words to him on their last visit, two days before the old man had suffered the massive heart attack and died instantly. That had been six months ago.

Take back your life.

Emilio's challenge rolled through Raoul's mind the way it had so often over the half year. Easy to say. A lot harder to do. But if he didn't take it back, he might wind up like Alma and Carlos, existing solely in the past, their lives stopped years ago like a clock on a sunken ship.

Raoul pulled on his jeans and sneakers, grabbed a flashlight and his windbreaker and left the boat. For once there was no sign of Tamale.

Once Raoul reached the sandy beach, he started to jog. Jogging was better than walking. It made it easier not to think. He ran until he neared the courtyard, then stopped, his mind consumed again with thoughts of Jaci—and his stomach churning with guilt.

Damn! No wonder the old nightmare had been so vivid tonight. He felt guilty for feeling any kind of attraction for another woman. It was irrational. Life had to go on. Wasn't that what he'd just been telling Carlos?

Raoul kicked off his shoes, rolled up his pant legs and waded into the water. The sand collected between his toes, then washed away with the receding tide. He was almost knee-deep when he heard the scream and knew it had come from the direction of the courtyard.

Jaci.

He didn't bother collecting his shoes before he took off at a dead run, his heart pumping like mad.

Chapter Eight

Impulsively, Jaci's hand flew to her mouth in a failed attempt to stifle her scream. The body of the young boy was floating just below the surface of the murky pool, face up, grotesquely swollen.

The wind stirred the water, and the body seemed to dissolve momentarily before coalescing again a few feet away, in the deeper water.

Tamale growled, low and threatening, but now he'd moved from the edge of the pool and was crouched at her bare feet. A million frightening questions ran through her mind, while her stomach rolled in protest at the gruesome image. Who was the boy? Where had he come from? How long had his body been floating in the pool? Why had no one missed him?

Shock took a back seat to her training, and she knelt to get a better look. The wind picked up, and shadows from the swaying palm fronds skulked across the scum, seemingly swallowing up the body. A dizzy spell hit without warning, and she closed her eyes for a second to clear the blurring. When she opened them again, the body had vanished.

"What's the problem? You hurt?"

She looked up to find Carlos hurrying toward her, barefoot and pulling on a shirt over his half-zipped, baggy slacks. Apparently he'd been asleep in the villa when he'd heard her scream. Tamale jumped up and ran to meet him, while Jaci grabbed a steadying breath.

"I'm okay," she said quickly, "but someone drowned in the pool."

"What the devil are you talking about?"

"There's a body of a young boy here. I don't know when he drowned, but from the looks of it, the accident happened several days ago, maybe longer."

Carlos threw his hands up in disgust. "You scared me half to death with that scream. I can't believe you woke me up for this."

He must not have heard her right. "A boy drowned in the pool. His body is still in there."

"Sure it is. Probably a ghost or two wandering around the beach, as well."

Frustrated and angered by his reaction, she bit back a sarcastic comment of her own. It was obvious from his changed attitude that Raoul had told him why she was on the island, but even that didn't justify his reaction to this. She turned at the sound of new footsteps approaching.

This time it was Raoul, dashing through the arched opening from the beach. He looked from Jaci to Carlos, then back to her again. "What's wrong? I heard a scream."

"Jaci is seeing things," Carlos answered for her.

"I saw the body of a young boy floating in the pool. It was as clear as..." She stopped, suddenly inundated by cold chills and doubts. The courtyard lighting was dim. The water was a soup of decomposing leaves and limbs. Under those circumstances, nothing should have been as clearly defined as the body had been.

Carlos walked to the edge and peered downward. "There's nothing in there but trash." He knelt, reached into the water and pulled a soggy rubber ball from the scum as if to prove his point. "Is this what you saw?"

"No, of course not." She scanned the pool again. There was nothing that even resembled a body. "I didn't make this up," she insisted. "I'm a professional, and I know a body when I see one."

"Okay, just settle down," Raoul said, his voice much quieter and calmer than either hers or Carlos's. "Exactly where did you see the body?"

"There." She pointed. "But I don't see it now."

"'Cause it's not there," Carlos said, "no more than any of the other ghosts people have seen out here have been. It's that damn documentary."

Raoul turned away from the pool and walked over to stand beside Jaci.

"I don't know what documentary you're talking about," she said, "and I don't believe in ghosts."

"Good," Raoul answered, aiming the beam of his flashlight into the water. He circled the pool, searching every crevice and corner as best he could without actually getting into the disgusting soup.

Jaci followed him, frantically searching for any sign of the body. The effort was wasted. Thoroughly confused and exasperated, she finally backed away and leaned against the courtyard wall. "This is useless. It's impossible to see through the scum in this light."

"I have to agree," Raoul said. "We'll have to wait until sunup before we come to a firm conclusion. But no matter what we find, the pool should be drained and cleaned."

"I'll give that some thought," Carlos said, though his tone lacked conviction. "But there's no use standing out here yakking about it now. If there's a body—which there isn't—it's not going anywhere tonight."

Tamale followed Carlos back to the villa. Raoul stayed. "Want to talk about it?" he asked, once his great-uncle had disappeared inside the villa.

"You don't have to humor me, Raoul. I'll be fine," Jaci said.

"I don't see how asking if you want to talk is humoring you. I just thought that since we're both wide-awake, we might as well keep each other company."

It was tempting, but she couldn't just

sweep their earlier confrontation from her mind. "Does keeping me company involve repeating your earlier ultimatum?"

"I still think you should leave, maybe now more than ever, but I'll work at keeping this a friendly conversation if you will."

She didn't feel particularly friendly or hospitable, but she wasn't too keen on being alone, either. She hesitated.

"It's not that big a deal, Jaci. The offer was only for conversation. You can kick me out whenever you want."

She took another look at the pool and felt the icy chill again. "In that case, I appreciate the offer." Turning, she padded toward the apartment, no longer sure that coming to Cape Diablo had been a good idea, but more determined than ever to see this through.

RAOUL KNEW HIS SPUR-OF-THE-MOMENT offer to stay and talk had been a mistake the moment he stepped inside Jaci's tiny apartment. Outside, she'd been vulnerable and unsure, and he'd felt the overwhelming urge to come to her rescue. Inside the cozy setting, alone with a woman he was unnervingly attracted to, he was the one on shaky ground.

"How about a cup of tea," she asked, "or would you rather have wine? Though I would have bought some hard liquor with me if I'd known things were going to turn out like this."

"I have plenty on the boat if you need it, but tea sounds good."

He followed her into the kitchen. The lemon-yellow color of her nightshirt was much more vivid under the bright indoor lighting, bringing her auburn hair and emerald eyes to life. The soft cotton shirt fell about halfway down her thighs, showing off her shapely legs while her bare feet highlighted her bright red toenails.

She set the teakettle over the burner, then reached to the top shelf of the pantry for the tea canister. The nightshirt rode a couple of inches higher, and everything inside him seemed to tighten and yet be shaky at the same time.

He'd have to work hard to keep this light and impersonal. He walked over to the counter where she was setting a couple of pottery mugs. "Can I help?"

"Not with the tea, but if you can shed any light on what just happened in the courtyard, I'd be grateful."

He settled into one of the four mismatched chairs around the small oak table. "Does that mean you're no longer convinced there's actually a body hidden somewhere under the muck?"

"I agree it's unlikely, and that it could have been shadows playing tricks on my eyes. I'd still like it checked out fully tomorrow morning."

"That makes sense. How did you happen to be out there this time of the night?"

"Tamale woke me. When I opened the door to see what was wrong, I saw him standing at the edge of the pool, growling and crouched as if he were in attack mode."

"So you went out to check?"

"First I called to him, but when he stayed put and started barking loudly, I thought he must be watching a frog or maybe even a snake. I figured if I didn't do something to settle him down, he'd never get quiet."

"Did you find a frog or a snake?"

"No. When I looked into the pool, I saw the body floating near the edge."

"And you saw it clearly?"

"The image was distinct. The features of the boy were distorted, swollen out of shape."

"But you didn't think there was a chance the boy was alive?"

"If I had thought that for a second, I would have jumped in and pulled him out. He was definitely dead, and had been for quite a while."

"So you screamed, and Carlos came to the rescue?"

"He showed up. I wouldn't call it a rescue. Evidently he has a whole new attitude toward me now that you told him why I came to Cape Diablo."

"How would you feel if people were constantly prying into your past?"

"I'm not prying, and this isn't about him. I'm conducting an investigation."

"For a project, not because you're a cop or that this is your job."

"You said you weren't going to lecture."

"Touché. Go ahead."

"At any rate, you heard most of the discussion, since you showed up only a minute or two after Carlos did." She turned and looked Raoul in the eye. "Where were you, anyway? Obviously not on the boat or in the boathouse?"

"I couldn't sleep so I took a walk on the beach."

"Seems to be a lot of insomnia on Cape Diablo."

"I have that trouble everywhere."

"I don't, and I've never seen a ghost, either, or a body that wasn't there, for that matter."

He studied her movements as she dropped a couple of tea bags into the mugs and poured boiling water over them. Graceful. Youthful. He was reminded again that she was probably ten years younger than he was.

He forced his mind back to the topic at hand. "Were you telling the truth when you said you haven't seen the documentary Carlos was talking about?" he asked, determined to get to safer ground.

"Why would I lie?"

"I'm just asking."

"I've never even heard of it."

"But you do know Andres Santiago's son drowned in the pool?"

"I read the police reports regarding the death."

"Then you probably know more than I do."

"I don't know much. The reports were sketchy. They stated that the boy was four years old at the time of the drowning. He apparently wandered out of the house without anyone knowing it."

"Odd that he couldn't swim, with the pool so convenient."

"Both Alma Garcia and his stepmother said he was an excellent swimmer. They couldn't explain why he drowned—at least that's what was recorded by the investigating officer The only possibility was that he was weakened by a recent case of measles."

"Unexplainable seems to be the motto of Cape Diablo," Raoul said. "Who found the body?"

"Alma did. She'd been the children's nanny only for a couple of months at the time. The police reported that she was hysterical, kept saying how devastated his father would be."

"Where was Andres?"

"Away on business. The stepmother and the nanny were in charge of the children." Jaci picked up one mug and set it in front of him, then reached for the other and joined him at the table. "You think I imagined the body in the pool tonight based on what I'd read about the drowning, don't you?"

"What do you think?"

"I guess it's possible," she admitted, "but it didn't feel imagined. The body seemed very real, and so close I could have leaned down and touched it."

"But you didn't?"

"No. By the time I got my wits about me, it had drifted out of reach. And I have to admit that it did seem less defined then."

"Maybe finding Mac's body today had you upset."

"I've seen a lot of corpses during my training," she said. "They've never led to my imagining ones that didn't exist."

"Welcome to Cape Diablo."

She looked up from her tea, her eyes narrowed but telegraphing her doubt. "Don't tell me you believe the island is haunted."

"Not haunted, just eerie. It freaked me out big time when I was a kid."

"Did Alma Garcia roam the island in that white gown then the way she does now?"

"As far back as I can remember."

Jaci toyed with the handle of her mug. "Are Carlos and Alma lovers?"

Raoul had asked himself that question hundreds of times without coming to any definitive conclusion. "If they are, I've never seen any indication. It's more like he's her caretaker."

"But it seems strange to live on a deserted island with a member of the opposite gender and never have sex."

Raoul wasn't sure how they'd gone from dead bodies to sex, but this was definitely not a topic he wanted to get into with Jaci tonight. He downed the rest of his tea, then carried his empty mug to the sink.

"I should go," he said, "and let you get some sleep. That is, if you're certain you'll be okay alone."

"I'll be fine," she assured him. "I'm not going near the pool until sunup."

He walked to the door. She followed him. He stood with his hand on the knob, suddenly wondering why in hell he was walking away from a woman in a lemon-yellow nightshirt who looked vulnerable and seductive and—

And this was getting him nowhere.

"Thanks, Raoul."

"Anytime."

She leaned closer, and there she was, in his face, too tempting to resist. He touched his lips to hers. The kiss was light and quick, yet it sent a stream of fire through him that zinged all the way to his toes.

He backed out the door while he still could. He barely noticed the pool when he passed it. There were far scarier things rolling around in his mind.

Things like how badly he wanted to walk back in that apartment and finish that kiss. But stabs of guilt mingled with the desire, and he knew the past wasn't ready to let go of him just yet.

JACI HADN'T FALLEN ASLEEP AGAIN until the first rays of the sun had begun to melt away the grayness of dawn. Strangely, it hadn't been thoughts of the body in the water but memories of Raoul's lips brushing hers that took the most blame for keeping her awake.

The kiss had been surprising, but not nearly as unexpected as the titillating thrill that had coursed through her like a tidal wave. And it wasn't even that much of a kiss. More like a brush of lips that he'd backed away from before it got started.

The kiss had been a fluke, and so had her reaction to it—some kind of arousal brought on by her shaky emotional state. Wouldn't her mother have a field day with that explanation?

Not that any of it mattered. Jaci had far more important things to worry about than almost kisses. For one thing, it was pretty certain now that her imagination had been working overtime last night. And if that was the case, she had to get hold of her emotions immediately.

There was no place in forensics for that sort of hysteria. Her professor would be appalled. Carlos had been livid.

But as disapproving as the old caretaker had been last night, he'd come though this morning. He'd been hard at it a little after 7:00 a.m., scooping out trash with a long-handled net. He'd pulled out lots of gunk, but nothing that even resembled a body.

Jaci dropped into one of the white wicker chairs and began to flip through pages of notes she'd made on the Santiago family.

Her information about the children's mother was extremely limited and not all that reliable, having come from a series of articles written about Andres Santiago's involvement with the Central American drug culture, and published in a now defunct

South American periodical. Fortunately, Jaci read Spanish, though not all that fluently.

The mother of the Santiago children, the first Mrs. Andres Santiago, had died giving birth to their only son. The son became the joy of Andres's life.

Three and a half years later, Andres married Medina, the daughter of a Central American dictator who'd been overthrown in a military coup.

Her father, General Norberto, had been executed along with his wife and only son. Medina escaped only because Carlos Lazario, a first lieutenant in the general's army, managed to sneak her out of the capital.

Andres smuggled them both out of their war-torn country. A few weeks later, he'd married Medina and brought both her and Carlos to Cape Diablo.

Shortly thereafter, the eighteen-year-old Alma Garcia was brought to the island to become nanny for the three Santiago children. Her father, who'd worked for Andres, had been slain in a battle with pirates trying to take over a shipment of illegal drugs headed to Miami.

Jaci was once again struck by the irony that Alma Garcia and Carlos, the last to arrive, and with no blood ties to Andres Santiago, were the only ones who remained on Cape Diablo.

With them on her mind, Jaci walked to the window and stared out at the villa. Even in full daylight, it was easy to see how some people would believe the place haunted. It might have been grand in its day, but hurricanes, years of salty air, and high humidity had taken their toll on the structure. Some of the red tiles were missing from the roof and the shutters that remained were mildewed, the paint chipped and faded.

Now that she thought about it, the old villa itself had likely cast the eerie shadows that had fueled her imagination in the moonlight. Had she been a superstitious person, she might have believed the rambling building was trying to tell her something, or even that the boy who'd drowned in the pool so many years ago was reaching out to her.

She knew better. Dead victims didn't cry out for help. The authorities had to go in and ferret out every clue. That's why forensics was so important. And forensically speaking, she had no reason at all to suspect the drowning was connected to her project in any way. But she was also beginning to doubt that the photos of the blood splatters would be all that helpful, either.

Restless now, Jaci grabbed her sunglasses and baseball cap and walked outside, careful this time to lock the French doors behind her. A few minutes later she was jogging along the beach.

The sand beneath her feet was warm, the sun on her back downright hot. She was almost to the boathouse when she turned and started back toward her own apartment.

She slowed to a walk, then stepped into the surf to cool off. A school of minnows swam between her legs, and she paused to watch their swishing movements. She walked out until the water was knee high, not caring at all that an occasional wave splashed her very short shorts.

She imagined Reyna and Pilar playing in the surf and running along the beach—until that one bloody night when their lives had changed forever or perhaps been snuffed out.

Had they witnessed a murder, then been killed because of what they saw? Had they been kidnapped after their parents were murdered? Or had they…

Something stung Jaci's leg, and she jumped backward. Maybe seaweed, maybe the tentacles of a jellyfish. All part of a day in the gulf. A couple of seagulls screamed overhead, their calls joined by the low whir of a small cabin cruiser fifty yards offshore.

Her mind shifted gears, drifting back to the dinner she'd shared with Raoul on his boat—and to last night's kiss. What was there about the man that got to her? He was nice looking, handsome in a rugged sort of way, but she'd been seriously kissed by better looking men and hadn't felt so much as a quickening heart rate.

Last night's feathered kiss had left her breathless and leaning against the door for support while he'd calmly strolled away.

So what had she expected him to do? Stay and make passionate love with a woman who imagined bodies when there were none? He was probably making plans to get the hell off of Cape Diablo, if he hadn't left already.

She waded back to shore and turned deliberately away from the boathouse and dock and toward the villa and her own apartment.

Raoul was just another man. The kiss was just another kiss—or almost kiss. And she had a project to complete.

The big arched doors to the courtyard were a hundred or so yards away when she spotted Tamale trotting toward her with what looked like a clump of seaweed in his mouth.

"What do you have there, boy?"

Tamale's tail wagged like crazy as he dropped his treasure at her feet. A pair of glassy eyes peered through the seaweed. Jaci knelt and pushed the stringy green strands away, revealing the cracked face of a baby doll. It took several minutes to untangle the rest of the seaweed.

The doll's head, legs and one remaining arm were of rubbery plastic. The body had apparently been of cloth, but the stuffing had all spilled out of a rip in the fabric of the doll's belly. Only scraps of tattered material remained.

A few strands of wiry yellow hair were still stuck to the plastic scalp. And beneath it, at the back of the neck, were two letters painted onto the discolored plastic: *P. S.*

Immediately, Jaci thought of Pilar Santiago. But how could one of Pilar's dolls wash up on the beach thirty years after the child had last been here?

Besides, judging from the doll's condition and what Jaci knew about the effects of submersion in saltwater, she'd guess it had been in the water no more than a month or so.

She turned the doll over in her hands, pausing to study a smear of something on the cloth that looked a lot like old, washed-out blood.

Tamale nosed the doll.

"Sorry, boy. I know this is your treasure, but I need to take it with me." She gave him a good neck scratching that seemed to satisfy him, then picked up a piece of driftwood that lay nearby and threw it down the beach for him to retrieve.

They played throw and fetch the rest of the way to her apartment, while possible scenarios ran around in Jaci's mind, chasing clues with the same fervor Tamale exhibited for the driftwood.

Only one held promise for Jaci's investigation, and that was if she could prove this actually was Pilar's doll and Pilar's blood. It wasn't likely, but unlikely clues had solved a lot of tough cases.

Perhaps the doll had been in the villa all these years and only recently been tossed into the surf. But why would anyone have kept a doll so many years, only to throw it away now? And what else might someone have saved?

Jaci had to find a way to get inside the villa and snoop around without either Carlos or Alma knowing. If she got caught, they'd be furious and probably ban her from the island, but it was a chance she'd have to take. Too bad she hadn't come before the villa had been placed off-limits.

She tossed the driftwood for Tamale one last time, then jogged toward the courtyard, the doll firmly clutched in her left hand. She darted through the arched door, then stopped abruptly when she saw Raoul leaning against her doorway.

Her pulse quickened. "Were you looking for me?"

"Yeah. I have some bad news."

"What?"

"Mac Lowell didn't commit suicide. He was murdered."

"Oh, no. Who killed him?"

"That's the bad news."

Chapter Nine

Raoul stood in the morning sunlight, staring at Jaci and wondering how he'd gotten himself so totally caught up in a situation that had disaster written all over it.

He could claim he was just being a Good Samaritan, but he knew it went deeper than that. Jaci got to him on several levels, not the least of which was the raw sensuality that caused the rock-hard feeling inside him right now.

She didn't look like one of those pale, thin models on the covers of fashion magazines, whose cleavage spilled out of their tops. She had the body for it, but she was more the girl-next-door type. Ponytail. Freckles spattering across her nose. Hips softly curved beneath her wet shorts.

And fiery green eyes staring at him right now.

"How did you hear about Mac's murder?"

"I had a call from a Detective Ralph Linsky with the Everglades City Police Department."

"Did he say what led him to the conclusion that Mac's death wasn't a suicide?"

"Just that the autopsy indicated bruises and injuries inconsistent with someone taking his own life."

"What kind of injuries? Internal? External?"

"He didn't say."

"Were there any suspicious substances in his stomach or bloodstream?"

"He didn't comment on that, either."

"And you didn't ask him?"

"I'm just a layman, remember?"

"Exactly. So why did he call you with that information instead of me?"

Tamale ran up and dropped a piece of driftwood at her feet. When she ignored it, he started tugging at a dripping mess she held in her hand—a dilapidated doll. She shooed the dog away and shifted the object to her other hand, holding it out of reach.

"What is that?" Raoul asked, pointing to the doll.

"Just something that washed up on the beach."

"Then why did you keep it?"

"Don't change the subject, Raoul. Why did the detective call you instead of me?"

"He tried you first, but couldn't get a connection."

"That figures. So how did he get in touch with you?"

"I have a very expensive phone."

"I don't get it," she said, tossing her head so that a few more auburn locks slipped from her ponytail to dance about her cheeks. "How would he know how to reach you?"

"I gave the investigating officer my business card yesterday. All the information was on it."

Jaci batted at a wasp that came too close. "So who killed Mac?"

"Detective Linsky didn't admit it, but I got the distinct impression that he thinks you may be more involved in the crime than just finding the body."

"More involved?"

"Possibly a suspect?"

Jaci's eyes flashed, and her right hand flew to her hip. "No way."

"I guess we'll find out soon enough. The

detective is on his way to Cape Diablo as we speak."

"He's not wasting any time, is he?"

"Doesn't appear to be. You have a right to a lawyer, you know."

"Of course I know, but I don't need one. I can't be a suspect. I'm a forensics science student on a case."

"Exactly. You're a student."

"What's that supposed to mean?"

"That you're not official. You seem to keep getting that confused, but I'm certain Linsky won't."

"I'm official enough. Once I explain the situation to the detective, he'll drop any suspicion of my involvement in this—if he's ever had any."

Raoul nodded, though he didn't fully buy into her theory. Explaining had never been enough to satisfy cops when he'd encountered problems with ownership of sunken treasures. "Would you prefer to be interrogated in your apartment or on my boat?"

"I don't plan to be *interrogated* anywhere." She pushed her index finger into her chin. "But I do have police reports and my notes scattered all over my apartment, so

maybe I should talk with the detective on
your boat—that is, if you don't mind."

"If I'd minded, I wouldn't have offered.
Besides, they want to talk to me as well. I'll
let Carlos know what's going on so he won't
come barging into the meeting."

"He won't like it," Jaci said, her soft lips
drooping into a scowl. "He thinks I've
already caused enough trouble."

"Imagine that."

She ran her full hand across the front of
her shorts. "I'll have to get out of these wet
clothes and grab a quick shower, but I'll be
down shortly."

He watched as she walked toward her
apartment, aroused by the way the wet shorts
clung to her butt, and thinking he had to be
nuts to be falling this hard for a woman he
barely knew.

And wanting her all the same.

JACI SHOWERED AND DRESSED IN a pair of blue
cotton cropped pants and a white short-
sleeved polo shirt. Taking a quick look in the
mirror, she lifted her hair from her neck,
holding it in place a few seconds before letting
it fall back to her shoulders. She grabbed a

tube of lipstick and was just about to start painting her top lip when she stopped abruptly.

She'd never worried about makeup before when she was involved in crime work, and she wasn't about to let one almost kiss make her start with the feminine, flirty routine now.

She scanned the room for her sandals. One was near the table, where she'd left the doll. The other was hiding. Thankfully, she found it a few seconds later, tangled in the fringed border of the cream-colored chenille spread, where it had landed when she'd kicked it off.

Slipping into the shoes, she grabbed an apple from the refrigerator and her keys from the table. She glanced toward the third-floor window of the villa as she rushed out the door. Alma was there as always, keeping watch over everything that happened on her island of the damned.

DETECTIVE LINSKY WAS JUST UNDER six feet tall and about thirty pounds overweight, with most of his excess fat in the spare tire that hung over his belt. His graying hair was cut short, and his skin was so weathered by sun, wind and saltwater, the lines around his eyes and mouth looked as if they would break if he smiled.

His partner, Jack Paige, was at least ten years younger—probably around forty. He was short, lean, blond and the more personable of the two. At least that was Jaci's first impression of them. So far they were just past the introduction phase and still getting settled in the ship's cozy living area.

Jaci sat in the tan armchair. The detectives were on the striped sofa. Raoul straddled a deck chair he'd brought in for the meeting.

Neither Jaci or Raoul interrupted while Detective Linsky explained that bruises found on Mac's arms convinced them that he hadn't been a willing participant in the hanging. She was pretty sure they weren't telling everything, but then cops seldom did unless they were talking to other cops.

Ralph Linsky crossed a foot over his knee, giving the impression this was a friendly chat. "Can you tell us again why you were meeting Mac at his home?"

"I was supposed to meet him at Slinky's Bar. When he didn't show up, I walked to his house."

"And why were you meeting him at Slinky's Bar?"

"I explained all of this to the investigating officers at the crime scene. I'm sure you have it in your notes."

"I'd like to hear it from you."

She explained again, starting with her interest in the photos of the blood splatters and ending with the phone call she'd received from Mac Lowell.

"Who did you tell about your scheduled appointment with Mac?"

"No one."

Linsky arched his brows. "No one? Not even Raoul, when you asked him to take you to the island?"

"No, I only told him that I had an appointment with someone. I didn't mention Mac."

"I understand, seeing as Raoul is a relative of Carlos Lazario."

Raoul held up a hand to halt the questions. "What's that supposed to mean?"

"It doesn't matter," Jaci said, just wanting to get this over and done with. "Carlos had nothing to do with it. My investigation was a private matter."

"So no one knew you were going to talk

to Mac Lowell about the old Santiago mystery?"

"I didn't tell anyone. I don't know who Mac may have told. Except..."

"Except what?"

"I doubt this means anything, but my room was broken into the morning I was to meet Mac. Nothing of value was taken, but the piece of paper where I had written down Mac's name, phone number and the time and place I was to meet him was missing."

Linsky uncrossed his legs and propped his elbows on his knees, looking her straight in the eye. "Let me make sure I have this straight. Someone broke into your apartment and the only thing they took was information about Mac?"

"I don't know that they took it. It's just that I haven't seen it since then. It probably got mixed up with my notes when they were rifling through them."

"And you didn't think any of this was important enough to mention?"

"His death appeared to be a suicide."

"Did you find out who broke into your apartment?" Linsky asked.

"Since nothing was taken, I just assumed

it was Alma Garcia. She has problems and probably just wandered in. At any rate, I'm sure she didn't leave the island and murder Mac."

"We're just trying to get all the facts," Linsky said.

"With that in mind, can you tell me exactly how the phone conversation went between you and Mac?" Detective Paige asked, taking over from Linsky, who had pulled a black notebook from his pocket and was making notes fast and furiously.

"I can't tell you word for word."

"Then give me the gist of it."

Even though she was certain both detectives had the investigating officer's notes at their fingertips, she repeated the information.

"Are you aware that Mac Lowell quit the force one week after the Santiago disappearance?"

"I read that somewhere."

"Yep, just packed up and left Everglades City without bothering to sell his house or his boat or his car, which he also left behind."

"I wasn't aware of that."

"He did. Just caught a plane and disappeared. Actually lived outside the country for several years, bought a house somewhere in the Caribbean Islands."

Raoul took the bait, likely to keep the detective from going on and on. "What did he do for money?"

"The police department always wondered that same thing."

"Mac's partner was killed about that same time," Linsky added. "Killed by a car bomb."

"Not according to police reports issued at the time of his death," Jaci said, sure she'd read that he had died in a car accident in Miami.

"Exactly."

"So why were the reports falsified?"

"So that his wife and kids, who were also reportedly killed in the car *accident,* had a halfway decent chance of starting all over again under assumed identities. Are you beginning to get a picture here, Miss Matlock?"

"Hard to miss with you painting it so vividly. You think someone paid off Mac Lowell to keep him quiet, and killed his partner when he couldn't be bribed."

"You are smart," Linsky said, "just like your professor said."

She groaned. "You talked to him?"

"Just checking out your credentials." Linsky shifted as if he couldn't quite get comfortable. "I know this all makes for a juicy project for your thesis, Miss Matlock, but under the circumstances, I think it best if you choose another one. Believe me, your professor understands that working on this case may very well have placed you in danger."

"Exactly how do you plan to protect Jaci now that you think she's in danger?" Raoul asked.

"I'm trying to get her off Cape Diablo. If she gives up the investigation and gets away from here, I doubt anyone will bother her."

"But you don't know that?"

"I can't guarantee it, but…"

"So whatever she decides, she's on her own."

Linsky shrugged off the comment. He and Paige stayed another thirty minutes, questioning Raoul about his relationship with Jaci. Neither cop looked convinced that the two of them were basically strangers. By the time the officers stood to leave, her head was pounding.

She walked with Raoul and the detectives onto the deck.

Linsky paused before stepping to the dock. "I'm not sure who killed Mac, but I do know those high-ranking drug guys order murders with the same calm you might swat a mosquito. And we have reason to believe that in spite of numerous arrests, smugglers and drug dealers still use the deepwater cove on the southern end of Cape Diablo. It's the perfect spot to stay hidden until they're ready to hit the open waters of the gulf."

If he was trying to frighten her even more than she already was, he was doing a darn good job.

When they left, Raoul put his hands on both her shoulders, massaging her strained muscles with the tips of his fingers.

She should leave, but she hated to go back to her apartment alone, hated to pass the swimming pool or to walk into the shadow of the villa and see Alma staring down at her. Hated the thought that Mac had been murdered.

"Let's take the boat out," she said, surprising herself with the request.

"Out where?"

"Out of sight of Cape Diablo. Someplace where I don't feel as if Alma's gaze is boring into me. Somewhere I can think, and try to digest all that Linsky had to say, without having it colored by the island's eerie atmosphere."

"You've got it."

Raoul squeezed her shoulders one last time, then went to start the boat. It occurred to her as the motors hummed to life that she had become totally trusting of a man she knew almost nothing about.

That couldn't be wise. Yet he was the only person she wanted to be with right now.

A SHARP PAIN SLID BETWEEN Carlos's ribs, so strong he had to hold on to the edge of the table for support until it passed. He started to take one of the pain pills he'd had smuggled out of Mexico, then decided against it. The pain would get much worse before this was over, and the illegal drugs were getting harder to come by.

Bull was not nearly as accommodating as Pete Trawick had been while he was running the supply boat. Bull didn't want trouble with the law. Carlos could appreciate that. But he needed the drugs to see him through this and to make the ending work as he had planned.

What he didn't need was the Santiago investigation reopened. Not that the cops would waste much time on the old crime. Truth was they hadn't been all that interested when it was fresh. Still, they would upset the *señora,* and he didn't need that.

She had been right to fight having tenants on Cape Diablo. He'd welcomed the change at first, had thrived on the new voices, the chance to talk.

The world had changed in the years since he'd moved to the island. Only he and the *señora* had stood still, except that they'd aged—and grown lonelier.

Slowly, he bent and pulled the small box from beneath the bed. He set it on the table and opened it, taking out the top letter.

The envelope was old and yellowed, the edges frayed from the hundreds of times he'd read it and all the others he'd kept. He slid the letter from the envelope and read the greeting.

"Mi querido."

My dear one...

Tears filled his eyes so that the words on the page ran together. It didn't matter. He knew the letter by heart. It was the last one she'd ever written to him.

He shook the old memories from his mind at the sound of someone on the stairs leading to the boathouse, and quickly hid the letter. The visitor was the *señora*. Her footsteps and voice were as familiar to him as his own.

There was a quickness in her steps today. He hoped that didn't mean she was on one of her frequent wild and frenzied escapes from reality. He never knew what would happen when one of those hit. No one did. No one ever had. Another reason he was glad the villa was off-limits to tourists now.

The door flew open and the *señora* stormed inside.

"Why were the police here?"

"They were friends of Raoul's. They just came by to visit him."

"Don't lie to me. They were here to see Jaci Matlock."

"Then you know more than I do."

"Get rid of her, Carlos. I want her off this island tonight. I want Raoul off as well. If you don't take care of it, I'll have Enrique do it."

"No. I don't want Enrique involved in this. They'll be off soon, but you must let me handle this. Do you understand?"

"Then handle it."

There was no reasoning with her when she was like this. It would serve her right if he did as Raoul wanted and left her all alone.

"Don't you trust me to take care of things, *señora?* After all these years, don't you trust me yet?"

"I trust you, Carlos. It's just that…" She met his gaze and trembled. "The police make me afraid."

He reached out and pulled her thin frame into his arms. "I'll take care of things," he whispered. "I promise."

And Carlos Lazario had never once gone back on a promise. She above all people should know that.

THE WIND WAS ALMOST nonexistent, and the water was as calm as Raoul had seen it in weeks, the perfect day for cruising the open waters of the gulf.

He needed this today. Needed to run the engines at full throttle and let the *Quest* fly. Needed the exhilaration of power and the feel of the wind in his face. He'd always been better at handling problems when he'd been out on a boat, almost as if the endless rolling waves helped put things in perspective.

But he'd spent little time on the boat over the last two years. It held too many memories of good times he'd shared with Allison.

The familiar guilt welled in his chest, and he closed his eyes, willing her image to coalesce in his mind. It had haunted him constantly in the first weeks and months after her death, but it formed more slowly now, and the features were growing less distinct every day.

Oh, he remembered the Allison in the pictures just fine. He had constant reminders of how she looked in them. Allison as she'd appeared coming up from a dive. In the mornings when she awoke, or stepped out of the shower, those were the images he had to work to hold on to.

They'd been so much alike. Had the same interests. Been almost the same age, with both of them raised by their grandparents. It made sense to fall in love with her, and Raoul had done it right, letting the attraction build slowly as they got to know each other.

Nothing like the way it was with Jaci. She was a good ten years younger than him. She was just starting her career, excited about evidence instead of sunken treasure. She studied DNA and blood splatter instead of routes of ships that had been lost at sea.

But there was no denying the attraction that sizzled between them. He turned his gaze in her direction, though he'd been avoiding that since she'd spread a multicolored beach towel over the padded bench and settled in to catch some rays.

She stirred and her perky breasts pushed against the fabric of her cotton shirt as she stretched and pulled her oversize sunglasses from her face.

She gave him a wave and dropped her long, shapely legs over the side of the bench. "I'm going inside for a diet soft drink. Can I bring you something?"

"I'm getting hungry," he said. "I'll come inside with you, and we'll rustle up some lunch."

"Great."

He slowed the twin engines. There was no idling the roaring inside him. He steered the boat back to the last island they'd passed, then dropped anchor and joined her in the cabin.

He stopped short when he saw Jaci near the bookcase, holding the picture of Allison.

"She's beautiful," Jaci said.

"Yeah. She was."

"Was?"

"She's dead."

"I'm sorry. Was she your wife?"

He hesitated, but there was no real reason to avoid the truth. He walked over, opened the cupboard, took out a bottle of Scotch and poured himself two fingers of the malt whiskey. Nothing about this was going to be easy.

Chapter Ten

Jaci waited silently as Raoul downed half the liquor he'd just poured. She was already regretting that she'd asked about the picture. With all the problems she was facing, she didn't need to add Raoul's to her list.

Turning away from him, she set the photograph back on the shelf. "I didn't mean to pry."

"You didn't. Allison was my fiancée. She was killed in a diving accident while we were exploring a sunken sailing ship off the coast of Bali."

"So she was a treasure diver as well?"

"Yes, one of my crew members. That's how we met." He swirled the Scotch in his glass, staring into it. "We had plans to be married as soon as we raised that ship."

He finished his drink, then set the glass on the counter and pressed his fingers into his temples as if he were trying to keep the memories from exploding inside him.

Jaci tried unsuccessfully to think of something to say that didn't sound trite. "That must have been rough on you."

"Hasn't been a picnic."

"No, I'm sure it hasn't." She ached to lay a hand on his arm, but with their own relationship so new and tenuous, even that seemed presumptuous. The silence grew awkward between them.

Finally, he looked up and locked his gaze with hers. "Sorry you asked?"

"I am, but only because talking about it seems so painful for you."

"I'm not one for going on about bad things," he said, "especially things that can't be changed."

"No, but sometimes talking helps."

"So they say."

Jaci's thoughts went back to the way Allison had signed her photograph. "Love, always." Her "always" had ended way too soon.

Jaci wrapped her arms around her chest, chilly though the temperature had been comfortable only moments before. She should drop the subject, but felt she had to know more if she was going to understand Raoul. And all of a sudden it seemed extremely important that she did. "When was the accident?"

"Two years ago last July."

For a second she thought she hadn't heard him right. Two years and three months, yet he showed all the signs of being in the first stages of grief when he talked about her death.

"You must have loved her very much."

"I loved her. I've never thought about there being degrees of love."

Jaci was pretty sure there were. At least her mother hadn't appeared to love her father the way he'd loved her.

Jaci's mind went back to the very tentative brushing of lips between herself and Raoul, and wondered if it were possible that he hadn't been with a woman in over two years. If so, it might just be normal male urges she'd mistaken for chemistry on his part.

She pulled a can of soda from the cupboard. Raoul filled a glass with ice and handed it to her. "Are you sure you don't want something stronger? You had a rough morning even before I unloaded on you."

"Soda is fine."

"Then I guess we should think about lunch." He opened the refrigerator and moved a few cartons around to get a better look at the contents. "We ate the last of the luncheon meat last night, but there's bacon, cheese, milk, lemons, grapefruit." He stooped to open another crisper drawer. "A head of lettuce and a couple of tomatoes. How about a BLT? Or an omelet? That looks like it for choices. Guess I should restock before we return to Cape Diablo."

"BLT sounds great. Shall I fry or slice?"

"Your choice," he said, already retrieving supplies from the fridge.

"Then I'll slice," she said. "If there's one thing I've learned in forensics, it's that it's better to be the one with the weapon."

"You obviously haven't seen my frying pan."

Raoul actually smiled as he pulled a cutting board and knife from one cupboard and a half loaf of wheat bread from another. It was good that his mood was brightening. Hers was probably going to dip to morose when they started talking about how her project du jour had turned into the assignment from hell.

RAOUL FELT AS IF HE'D BEEN battered by a two-by-four from the inside out as he turned the slices of thick, hickory-smoked bacon. Today was the first time he'd said Allison's name out loud in months. It had been just as painful as Jaci had thought, but for all the wrong reasons.

Not that he didn't still miss her. Part of his heart would always belong to Allison. But the guilt wouldn't let up. It just sat there and festered like the cancer inside Carlos must be doing.

If Raoul could live that one day over, he'd change everything about it. But there was no way in heaven or hell he could nullify his actions or redeem his mistakes.

Jaci reached around him to set the knife into the sink. She brushed against him in the process, and his awareness level jumped so high he almost dropped the fork.

He couldn't imagine what he was thinking when he'd suggested they cook together. The kitchen was too damn small to share with her. He should have learned that the other night.

Jaci scooted past him to return the remainder of the lettuce to the refrigerator. "Did you say you have cheese?"

"There's a chunk of cheddar in the meat tray."

"Good. I like cheese on my BLT, and lots of mayo. What about you?"

Right. Take the cues from her. Keep this light and get through it without taking her in your arms and making a fool of yourself.

"Cheese, mayo and a big sour pickle on the side."

"Yuck. I hate sour pickles."

"Don't know what you're missing."

She started humming while she spread mayo on the slices of wheat bread that had just popped from the toaster. Humming in the face of danger was probably a good quality for a forensics scientist, not that he was certain exactly what a forensics scientist did.

He yanked some paper towels from the roll and laid them in a plate to absorb the excess grease. "Aren't there separate fields of study for forensics experts, kind of like specialties for doctors?"

"All kinds of specialties. For example, forensic dentists cast evidence like bite marks."

"So the cops knew who bit into a steak?"

"Or took a bite out of their victim. There's also forensic botany, entomology and anthropology, to name a few."

"Do you have a specialty?"

"DNA analysis and blood splatter."

"Which explains why you were so interested in talking to Mac Lowell."

"Exactly. Blood splatter is mainly used to determine the location of impact and what type of weapon was used in violent crimes. For example, a baseball bat would leave a different pattern than a knife. A bullet from a .38 is different from one from an Uzi."

"You sound as if you know your stuff."

"I've worked hard to learn it. I'm proficient in all kinds of basic criminology, but my real interest is solving crimes that have little or no obvious evidence. I like a challenge."

Raoul speared the crisp bacon slices and deposited them on the waiting paper towels. "So will you work with the FBI after you graduate?"

"I'm not sure. I have several other options."

"Such as?"

"I can be a police criminologist or I could work for defense attorneys, disproving all the evidence against their clients. That's probably where the most money is—and sometimes the fewest ethics."

"Which way are you leaning now?"

Jaci placed the bacon on the sandwiches. "Toward a position with a police department in a major municipality like Miami or Los Angeles, where they get a huge variety of crimes to solve."

Big cities versus lonely oceans—another major difference between them, not that Raoul was counting.

"Let's eat outside again," Jaci said, grabbing her plate and soda and leading the way. "I always think better in the sunshine. It's from being raised a Florida girl."

"Outside it is," he said, grabbing his own food and following her. Guilt, food, sunshine, Jaci—and murder. You'd think that would kill a man's appetite, but he was famished.

Obviously Jaci was, too. They were half finished their meal before she broke the silence.

"My turn to ask questions," she said. "Don't worry. They're not personal."

"Okay, shoot."

She scooted closer to the small table that separated them. "There are dozens of theories about what happened the night the Santiagos disappeared, but as a guy with ties to the island, what do *you* think happened that night?"

Raoul saw no reason not to hand it to Jaci straight. "I think they were all murdered."

"You say that with conviction."

"Why not? Andres Santiago led the kind of life that begot violence."

"But how do you explain that there were no bodies, and their yacht was missing, as well as the treasure Andres had supposedly buried on the property?"

"Don't tell me you think Andres just gathered up his family and treasure and sailed away in the night. That he gave up his life of crime and took on a new identity on some foreign shore, leaving blood splattered all over the boathouse to throw off anyone who might come looking for him."

"It could have happened like that."

"If you believed that for one moment, you would never have chosen this as your project."

She nodded. "You're right. I agree with you. I've always thought the blood in the boathouse was Santiago blood. And after coming to Cape Diablo, I'm even more convinced."

"Why is that?"

"I don't believe in black magic or evil spirits or any of that, at least I never did before. But Cape Diablo has an unmistakably sinister feel to it, as if the deadly secrets are crying out for someone to uncover them." She shuddered and pushed aside the plate holding the last few bites of her sandwich. "How's that for creepy?"

"It's the isolation," Raoul said. "You're not that far away from the mainland, but when you're surrounded by nothing but water and countless islands that run together like spilled green paint, it seems that you're at the end of the world."

Jaci got up and walked to the railing. The sun glistened on her wind-tousled hair, and a hard knot settled in his gut.

"You've got more to deal with than the island's aura, Jaci."

"I know." She turned back to face him. "Do you remember the doll I was holding when you came to tell me that Detective Linsky was on his way?"

"You said Tamale came out of the sand dunes with it in his mouth. Things wash up all the time. Carlos pulled up the handlebars of a tricycle with his crab traps this morning."

"The doll had 'P. S.' painted on the back of its head."

P. S. Pilar Santiago. He could almost see the wheels turning in Jaci's mind.

"Get real, Jaci. If that doll had been swimming with the fishes for thirty years, it would likely be on the other side of the world by now—if there was anything left of it."

"I don't think it was in the water that long, but I'm sending it in to the university forensics lab for study. I especially want them to test a stain on the doll's dress that looked as if it could be blood."

"Do you have a sample of Pilar's DNA for comparison?"

"No, but thorough testing can determine if the stain is actually blood, and approximately how long the doll has been in the water."

"You've had your head in too many textbooks."

"No. Think about it. Suppose someone here on Cape Diablo only recently decided that the doll could be incriminating. They could have thrown it into the waves thinking that would be the end of it, but instead it washed right back to the island."

Someone on Cape Diablo. Irritation hit, fast and furious. "Carlos would never kill anyone, especially not two little girls. And it's damn unlikely that Alma killed four people and got rid of the bodies without an accomplice."

"Maybe there was an Enrique in her life back then. We don't know."

"You told me once you didn't fabricate evidence, but it sure sounds like you are to me. Which would be fine for your project if that's all that was at stake. But it's not."

Raoul pushed back from the table and walked over to stand beside Jaci at the rail. "Give it up. Go back to the mainland before you end up dead."

Defiance flared in her green eyes. "I can't do that."

"Why the hell not?"

"It's not just a project, Raoul. It might have been in the beginning, but...I can't explain it, but I have to find the answers. To do that, I need to get inside that villa."

"Don't go snooping in there alone."

"Surely they don't shoot trespassers on Cape Diablo."

"I'm serious, Jaci. I don't want you going in there by yourself. If you have to see the place, I'll go in with you. Let me talk to Carlos about it first."

"He'll say no."

"Then I'll work something out. Promise me you won't go in solo."

"I appreciate the offer."

"How about a better one? Let me take you back to the mainland tonight, and *I'll* do your research here. All you have to do is give the orders."

"And what kind of cop will I make if I give up every time there's a little danger?"

"A live cop."

"If there are answers to be found on Cape Diablo, I'm going to find them."

God, he'd love to shake some sense into her. "Do you hear yourself, Jaci? You know the danger, but you'll risk your life to be the woman known for solving the Santiago case?"

She looked up at him, and this time he saw more than defiance. He saw conviction—and traces of fear.

"I can't give up, Raoul, but it has nothing to do with gaining a reputation. It has to do with who I am. My father was the best damn cop in Florida, and if I'm going to be one, I'm going to be like him. That's the passion that drives me. It's who I am, and I'm sorry if you can't understand that."

Driving passion. God, he wished he didn't understand it, wished he hadn't lived it. Wished it hadn't cost him so much.

"This isn't your life, Raoul, but it is mine. You can go anytime. I have to stay."

But it wasn't that easy. He had no idea where his feelings for Jaci were going, but he knew he couldn't walk away.

"If I can't persuade you to give this up and go back to the mainland, then I'm moving into the pool house apartment above yours."

She moved her right hand so that it fitted over his. "You don't have to do this, Raoul."

"I know. I want to." The words escaped around a knot in his throat.

"Thanks."

She leaned in closer and touched her lips to his.

He hadn't initiated the kiss, but once it started, he was helpless to fight it.

He didn't try to think about why anymore. He just pulled her into his arms and let his breath and desire tangle with hers until he was so weak with wanting he could barely stand. Every part of him was on fire when she finally pushed him away.

"I think we should go back," she said.

He struggled to catch his breath. "Yeah."

Reluctantly, he released her. Going back was the smart thing to do. His mind agreed. His body protested painfully.

And he wondered how he'd ever make it sleeping just above her through the long, dark night.

Chapter Eleven

Jaci found the haunting aura of Cape Diablo spookier than ever when they returned to the island. She dropped to the side of her own soft and slightly lumpy mattress and impulsively ran her tongue across her lips, hungry for even a lingering trace of the taste of Raoul.

The last thing she'd expected to find on Cape Diablo was a man who'd get to her the way he did. This would be the very worst time in her life to begin a relationship. She was just starting her career. Raoul was getting over— or *not* getting over—the loss of his fiancée.

Jaci walked to her desk and picked up the copy of the police report filed the morning after the Santiago family had disappeared. Nothing like immersing herself in a good police report to forget everything else.

It didn't work this time, but she kept reading, determined to find some clue she'd overlooked the first two dozen times she'd read it. She studied the passages she'd highlighted.

The villa itself showed no signs of struggle. The bed in the master bedroom was mussed, but only on one side. One of the twin beds in the girls' room also looked as if it had been slept in. The mattress on the other bed was bare. The sheets, blanket and pillow had been stripped.

One of the girls' beds slept in. The other stripped. Had they huddled together in one narrow bed when they'd come home from the celebration or had the beds been left that way from the morning before?

Pilar, the younger had been eight, probably too old to wet the bed, though some children did still have accidents at that age. She could have spilled something, maybe a glass of milk or fruit juice.

But if it was blood that had caused the bed-covers to be stripped, it would mean the girls were stolen from their beds that night, and not taken hostage when they'd stepped from the yacht, as a lot of people had hypothe-sized.

But if the family was already in the villa when the killers struck, why was the blood in the boathouse?

Jaci walked to the French doors just in time to catch a glimpse of Alma hurrying through the arched opening that led to the beach. She was wearing a long, flowing skirt and a white peasant blouse, and looked much younger than she did in the tattered dress she wore to roam the island at night.

Jaci watched until she disappeared from sight, a plan already taking shape in her mind. Carlos had asked Raoul to come to the dock, where he and Enrique were taking apart his ailing motor. Alma was somewhere on the beach. This was just the opportunity Jaci had been waiting for. Raoul wouldn't like it, but it was what she had to do.

She ducked out the door and ran across the rough brick courtyard, not stopping until she reached the heavy wooden door at the front of the house. She wrapped her hand around the doorknob and twisted. It didn't budge.

Jaci took a step back and looked up at the

moss and vine covered walls and the wrought-iron railing that bordered the second-floor loggia. One of the doors leading to the balcony stood open, taunting her.

This would be easy with a ladder. There was none in sight and no time to go looking for one. Her gaze fastened on the old, tangled bougainvillea vines that climbed up the faded stucco walls. They weren't strong enough to support her whole weight, but that didn't mean she couldn't use them.

Kicking off her sandals, she stuck a toe into the first louvered slot of an aging green shutter. One foot and then another. It really wasn't all that difficult as long as she used the vines to stabilize herself. She didn't look down until she'd managed to hoist herself over the railing.

Once there, she wasted no time in scooting through the open door and into a dark, moldy hall. She trembled and shrank against the cold wall. The feeling of evil that seemed to shroud the island was a hundred times stronger inside the villa, almost as if it were a living, breathing substance.

Raoul had been right. She shouldn't have come alone. But she had, and now she had to suck it up. She started walking, and her movements did as much as her mental pep talk to help her get past the groundless fear.

The bedroom that Pilar and Reyna had shared was on the second floor, with a large window overlooking the beach. That bit of information hadn't been included in the police report, but had been mentioned in one of the articles written later about the Santiago family.

Another article had included a map of the house by someone who'd claimed to be a friend of Medina's. Jaci didn't have the map with her, but she had a mental picture of the second floor filed away in her mind.

She stopped at the stairwell to the third floor to get her bearings. A circle of light shone down from the upper story and Jaci picked up the faint strains of a waltz from the radio or perhaps a CD that Alma left playing. She imagined the grey-haired woman up there dancing with her imaginary lover night after night, the same way she danced on the beach.

The urge to take the stairs to the third floor was strong, but she needed to see the girls' room even more. She rushed past three doors, all closed. Finally she reached the last room on the western side of the house, the one said to be the bedroom shared by Reyna and Pilar.

"Please don't be locked," she whispered as she turned the knob. And then her breath caught in her throat as the door creaked open and Jaci stepped back thirty years in time.

The room looked as if Pilar and Reyna had just gone downstairs for dinner and would be returning any second. The beds were turned down, the pillows fluffed, old-fashioned embroidered nightgowns ready and waiting for them to slip into. One pink. One blue. Jaci's heart constricted at the thought of the two little girls who'd never gotten to grow up.

The air in the room seemed musty and cold in spite of the sun that poured through the windows, painting squares of light across the beds and worn carpet.

Jaci surveyed everything, her gaze settling on an exquisite santo that dominated the small table separating the two beds. She picked up the statue of St. Thomas, amazed at its weight as she admired the skill of the artist and the small bits of jade, quartz and turquoise embedded in the heavy metal.

Her finger slid across the sharp edge of one of the stones as she returned the statue to its place of honor. A drop of blood formed on the tiny cut. Jaci blotted the blood on the inside of her shorts pocket and crossed the room to examine two child-size desks separated by a heavy, wooden bookcase.

Reading texts and math books were stacked neatly on the back corners of the desks, and there were pens and a pad of paper on each.

Two brightly painted music boxes shared the top shelf of the bookcase with an assortment of framed photographs.

Jaci picked up a picture of Andres Santiago and his two daughters. He, like the rest of the family, was easy enough to recognize, since she'd seen countless photos of them in the numerous articles she'd collected. Andres was as handsome and dashing in this one as he was in all the others.

She picked up another picture, this one in a heavy silver frame. Andres was standing with his arm around his new wife, who smiled up at him, either totally in love or faking it well. Pillar and Reyna were in front of them, clasping hands and looking like frothy angels in frilly white party dresses.

The white stucco gleamed in the sunlight
and the shutters in such disrepair now were
freshly painted and straight then, showcas-
ing the crimson cascade of bougainvillea in
full bloom.

But were looks deceiving? Had Andres
sensed some innate evil in the villa even
then, and simply taken his family and left in
the middle of the night?

And here she went again, imagining the
villa with powers it couldn't possibly
possess. Jaci shook her head. But the isolation could have gotten to Medina, and she
might have insisted he give up his life of
crime and flee to someplace they could live
a normal life. After all, she'd been only sev-
enteen when Andres had saved her from the
rebels who'd overthrown her father, and
brought her to Cape Diablo as his wife.

That had to be culture shock for her—going from being the beautiful and pampered
daughter of a dictator to living on an isolated
island with three children to care for.

Jaci scanned the other photographs,
stopping to admire Andres's yacht. It was as
impressive as the villa in its own way, but
sleek and modern for its time, while the villa

was timeless. A piece of bronzed scrollwork spelled out the name of the boat: *Conquiste.*

The only surprise was that there were no pictures of the girls' brother, who'd drowned. Maybe Andres and Medina had decided it was better for the girls' emotional state not to have constant reminders of the tragic drowning.

But then tragedy struck them, anyway. Maybe right here in this very room.

The beds were made now. That night they hadn't been. Had Pilar been killed in one of those very beds?

Jaci shuddered as an image burst into her mind. The bed was no longer empty and sunlight no longer poured through the window. The room was dark except for moonlight painted shadows on the walls and across the twisted sheets.

And there was Pilar, lying in a pool of blood, her doll cradled against her small, heaving chest. The young girl opened her eyes and stared blankly at the ceiling but her pale lips were moving. "Run, Jaci! Run or the wicked witch will kill you, too!"

A scream burned at the back of Jaci's throat, but wouldn't come out. She stumbled, then caught the bedpost for support. Her fingers slipped as if sliding though warm, sticky blood.

Perspiration wetted her underarms and crawled into the cleavage beneath her cotton shirt. She tugged at the damp fabric as vertigo hit with a vengeance, setting the room in motion.

Jaci didn't hear the warning of approaching footsteps until it was too late.

Chapter Twelve

"The villa is off-limits."

The gruff voice attacked the mental fog and Jaci blinked repeatedly, trying to clear her blurred vision and separate reality from the surreal.

Carlos was standing over her, his muscles flexed, his face twisted in anger. Fear and adrenaline flooded her bloodstream as she saw the santo raised in his right hand, as if it were a hammer ready to strike.

She scooted away from him, searching frantically for something she could use to defend herself. There was nothing within reach.

Slowly, he lowered the statue to his side, but his intimidating stance and burning glare didn't let up. "What are you doing here?"

She pushed herself to a standing position, head high, shoulders straight, struggling not let him see how shaken she was. "I just wanted to look around. The door wasn't locked."

"And you're a prying forensic scientist, so you think the rules were made for other people?"

"I didn't bother anything," she said, "and it's not as if the entire villa is a private residence. Mr. Cochburn said part of the second floor was rented out before the roof was damaged in a recent storm."

"It's not public now." Carlos stepped closer, the statue still gripped tightly in his hand. "Get the hell out. If I see you inside the villa again..." He let the threat go unfinished.

Her mind wouldn't let her do the same. He'd do what? Kill her to keep some murderous secret silent?

"What happened to the girls who once slept in this room, Carlos?"

He stiffened and his face turned bloodred. "I said get out."

She stepped out of his reach, nearer to the door, where she could escape if it came to that. She was certain she could outrun him. "Were Pilar and Reyna murdered that night? Were they killed in this very room?"

The veins in his neck and forehead popped out as if they were about to explode, while the muscles in his face stretched so tightly they appeared frozen. Only his eyes were alive, deep and dark—and tortured.

He knew. Whatever had happened to Pilar and Reyna, Carlos knew. Jaci was sure of it.

"Get out, Miss Matlock. Pack your things and be off the island by nightfall. I don't care if you have to swim, just don't be here when the moon comes up. If you are…"

"If she is, what?"

Jaci jumped at the sound of the voice, and she and Carlos both spun toward the door. Raoul was standing there glaring at his great-uncle.

"If she is, you'll do what?"

Carlos sputtered a couple of Spanish curse words beneath his breath, then slammed the santo down on the edge of the bedside table with such force that the old wooden tabletop splintered.

"I want her off the island," the older man said. He turned back to Jaci. "Get your things and Raoul can take you to the mainland."

"That's her decision," his nephew stated.

"So now you're on her side?"

Raoul stepped into the room and put a hand on his great-uncle's shoulder. "I don't see any call to choose sides. Jaci's a paying guest on Cape Diablo. She has a right to be here."

Carlos backed away from him. "So that's how it is? Blood means nothing to you."

"Don't make this into more than it is." Raoul spoke softly, clearly trying to diffuse the volatile situation. "Jaci may have strayed out-of-bounds, but there's no harm done. I'm sure the villa will survive her visit. It's survived far worse and has seen his share of tenants."

"The rules have changed." Carlos grunted and pointed a knotty, gnarled finger at Jaci. "She's only here to make trouble."

"The trouble at Cape Diablo started long before she arrived. I'm walking her back to her apartment, and then you and I are going to have a long talk."

"There's nothing to talk about. I've said my piece. I want her gone from here by nightfall."

Carlos turned and stomped away, only to stop at the door and double over, grabbing his stomach as if someone had punched him below the belt.

Raoul rushed to him. "You need to be in a hospital?"

Carlos didn't answer, but just shrugged him off and limped away. Jaci could tell from the receding footsteps that he wasn't moving too swiftly.

Raoul shook his head, looking as if he'd reached the saturation level for frustration and aggravation, but she could see the concern in his eyes when he met her gaze.

"What are you doing in here?"

"I saw Alma leave, and I took the opportunity to have a look around inside the villa."

"I thought we agreed to do that together."

"We talked about it. I never promised anything," Jaci reminded him.

"And Carlos stumbled across you when he came back to the villa to check on Alma," Raoul said. "You must have caught him by surprise."

"It was more than surprise. I thought for a minute he was going to smash my skull the way he did that table."

"He was just trying to frighten you. He wouldn't have actually hit you."

Raoul might believe that. She didn't, and she was the one who'd been the recipient of

Carlos's rage. "How did you get in? The door was locked."

"Carlos left it open. Are you okay?"

"Not really, but then I wasn't even before Carlos showed up on the scene."

"Why is that?"

"Look around you."

Raoul did, then let out a low, disbelieving whistle. "It's as if Pilar and Reyna just stepped out."

"Exactly. Alma has kept things just the way they were thirty years ago. How weird is that?"

"Probably no weirder than living out here in this decaying villa for three decades."

"I think it's a sign of more."

"Like what?"

Jaci took a deep breath and let it out slowly. "I think the Santiago girls were killed in this room and that Alma had something to do with the murders and…" She hesitated.

Raoul's eyebrows arched. "And what?"

"Carlos knows what happened." There was a good chance he might have been in on the murders as well, but she wouldn't throw that at Raoul just yet.

"Are you basing all that on the appearance of this room?"

"It's a proven fact that when a person is involved in a violent crime, either as a victim or a culprit, they sometimes find it impossible to move past the event. That's what Alma has done. She's kept time standing still, at least in her mind."

Raoul narrowed his eyes. "Why do I think there's more?"

Because there was. The images Jaci had visualized in this room had been so vivid, she would have sworn that Pilar had talked to her from the grave. But if Jaci admitted that to Raoul, he'd think she was as mentally unstable as they both thought Alma was.

"If there's more, it's the villa itself," she said, hating that a tremble crept into her voice. "It's only too bad these old stucco walls can't talk."

Raoul crossed the room and took her in his arms. She let him hold her, while her nerves went into meltdown.

He kissed the top of her head and ran his hands over her shoulders. "You've had a rough day. You need a glass of wine, a hot bath and some normalcy."

She didn't contradict him, but wine and a bath wouldn't change the facts. At the very least, Carlos knew the answer to the mystery that had hung over Cape Diablo for thirty years.

At the worst, Raoul's great-uncle had killed four people, including two innocent little girls. There wasn't a doubt in her mind he was capable of it, not after she'd seen such murderous rage burn in his eyes.

"Let's get out of here," Raoul said, leading her to the door, "before Alma returns and we have to deal with her as well."

Jaci looked back at the room one last time, and her gaze focused on the statue of St. Thomas, the same one that Carlos had raised against her. The perfect weapon. Convenient. Hard enough to crush a skull.

And with sharp edges on the jewels that could cut into the flesh and cause enough bleeding that it would spill onto the covers and the doll clutched in a small girl's hands.

Jaci's own blood ran cold at the new image.

"Are you sure you're okay?" Raoul asked.

"Yeah." She was fine for now. But would Raoul be if evidence were found that incriminated his aging great-uncle in a crime that would send him to prison for the rest of his life?

THE PAIN HAD DULLED. NOW it was just a nagging ache that camped in the pit of Carlos's stomach and hardened like a block of cement. He slapped a mosquito that was using his neck as its personal feeding trough, and wiped a stream of perspiration from his forehead.

He stopped and looked around. There wasn't an inch of the island he didn't know. Not a bog or a slough he hadn't stepped into. Not a bird, snake or animal he didn't recognize. Cape Diablo was his world, but he didn't seem to belong here anymore.

He'd turned south when he left the villa. He'd passed the old servants' quarters, and was already to the edge of a boggy swamp. Another hundred yards and he'd be at the deepwater cove that was once again a hotbed of drug smuggling activity.

Everything was spinning out of his control.

He'd made a mistake back at the villa. A very big mistake, but it could have been worse. He could have killed Jaci.

Then all the lies, all the secrets, all the horrible recollections that slithered through the black corners of his mind like a rattlesnake would have been for nothing.

Carlos leaned against the trunk of a cabbage palm and watched a purple gallinule that stared at him from a safe spot across a slough of greenish water. The bird belonged to the Gulf Islands the same way Carlos belonged to Cape Diablo.

Only the bird was a prisoner of his needs of survival. Carlos was a prisoner of fate.

He turned and started back to the boat-house, suddenly weary to the bone. He didn't stop until he neared the villa and saw the *señora* and Enrique walking side by side toward the beach.

The weariness changed to anger. If Carlos were going to kill anyone, it should be Enrique. In fact, he should have killed him years and years ago.

RAOUL WAS IN THE APARTMENT above Jaci's. She could hear thumping, as if he was moving furniture around. Jaci stood at the window, sipping the glass of chardonnay he'd poured for her, while troubling images played havoc with her reasoning abilities.

In spite of the images or the run-in with Carlos, Jaci wasn't sorry she'd gone into the villa. She only wished she'd made it to the third floor to explore Alma's quarters. *Next time,* Jaci consoled herself.

She was about to start the water for the hot bath Raoul had suggested when she spotted Alma walking across the courtyard, apparently returning from wherever she'd gone earlier.

Jaci was amazed again at how young she looked with her hair up, and dressed in normal clothes. She was walking fast, her thin arms swinging at her sides, her eyes straight ahead.

All of a sudden she slowed her pace and turned toward the pool, stopping at the edge to stare into the murky water. Her posture went rigid, except for her hands, which fisted and released in rapid succession.

There might be rules against guests wandering through the villa on their own, but there were none forbidding her to approach Alma Garcia in the courtyard.

Jaci was halfway across the courtyard when Alma stepped back from the pool. When she turned, Jaci got a clear look at her face. She was pasty-white and her eyes were wide open, though her stare was vacant, almost like that of a corpse.

A second later, Alma bolted and ran toward the villa, surprising Jaci with her speed.

Jaci walked to the pool and peered into the water to see what had frightened Alma. There was nothing there but the usual muck.

A boat horn sounded in the distance. It was likely Bull bringing the supplies and mail. Jaci rushed back inside for the package containing the doll.

"I'm off to the dock to meet the supply boat," she yelled loudly enough for Raoul to hear in the upstairs apartment.

"I'm right behind you."

HER OLD LUNGS WERE BURNING by the time she reached the third floor. She fell onto her worn sofa and held both hands against her heart to keep it from bursting right out of her chest. She closed her eyes tight, but still she saw Andres's small son lying on the bottom of the pool.

Carlos claimed she was losing her mind to the pills and the drugs. But how else did he expect her to survive? He didn't understand. Thankfully, Enrique did.

Her hands shook as she opened the drawer

by her bed and unlocked the metal box where she kept the stash Enrique had replenished.

If she was going mad, it wasn't from the drugs, but from Jaci and people like her who wouldn't just go away and leave her and Carlos alone.

They wanted answers, but answers wouldn't change anything. Nothing could ever undo what had happened that night. That's why she had to get rid of them. That's why she had to get rid of all of them, even Carlos.

One day she might have to get rid of Enrique, as well. But not yet. She needed his strength—and his drugs.

BULL LIFTED A BOX OF groceries onto the deck. "These are yours, Carlos."

The old man stooped on the edge of the dock and did a quick inspection of the contents. "Where's the rest of my order?"

"Didn't come in."

"I told you I needed it."

"It didn't come in," Bull said again, this time with an edge that meant he was through talking about it.

Carlos wasn't, but he didn't want to say more with Raoul and Jaci standing around.

"And these are your groceries, Jaci. Oh, yeah, and you got this letter, too." Bull pulled a big brown envelope from the mailbag inside his boat. "Looks official."

"Thanks, and I have something for you to post with FedEx the minute you get back to the mainland. It's extremely important that it gets to the addressee in the morning."

"You got it. How long you figure to be out here?"

"I'm not sure."

"Yeah, well, you take care of yourself. There's a storm brewing in the Gulf. You're going to get some rain tonight and plenty of it."

A big storm was brewing, that was for sure, but Bull didn't know the half of it. Carlos picked up his box and moved to where he could read over Jaci's shoulder. The letter was from the university lab. He waited for her to open it, but she just stuck it in the bag with her groceries.

Raoul reached for the box Carlos was holding. "Here, I'll carry those up the steps for you."

"I'm not helpless yet. You'd be better off helping the lady you're so worried about."

"I'll get hers, too, as soon as I get these up the stairs for you."

Carlos gave up the box. He wasn't really mad at Raoul, at least not since he'd cooled off a bit. If he'd been in his nephew's shoes up in the villa this afternoon, he'd have likely reacted the same way.

But he wasn't. He was in his own shoes. Worn shoes that had walked too many miles over the same damn, swampy turf.

He waited until Jaci left the dock, then walked down to the supply boat for a private word with Bull. He needed the necessary supplies to carry out his plans. Things were heating up fast.

He slid his hand into his jacket pocket and wrapped it around the pistol. That was his backup plan. If all else failed, it wouldn't.

JACI FOUND A PRIVATE SPOT, hidden away in a thick cluster of mangroves, before ripping open the brown envelope. She fully expected the report to verify her suspicions that Alma had broken into her apartment and likely taken the note about Mac, which had never shown up.

There was no way she'd gone to Ever-

glades City and murdered the former policeman, but she might have given the information to someone who had.

The first words leaped out at Jaci, even
though they were not part of the official
report: "You lucked out. But be very careful
out there in Weirdsville!"

The note was from a fellow forensics
student who worked in the lab. Jaci scanned
the report quickly, searching for pertinent
points. The most shocking part of the report
had nothing to do with Alma Garcia.

Fingerprints from a Miami arrest in a
barroom brawl thirty-five years ago were an
exact match for the large primary prints on the
book. Enrique Lopez was not who he
claimed.

"What are you reading, *señorita?* Perhaps
a letter from your lover?"

Her breath caught in her throat as Enrique
approached, and she folded the report
quickly and stuffed it back into the envelope.
"No. It's just some information."

Enrique stepped closer and a tingle of fear
skittered up her spine. She'd been uneasy
around him from the start, had felt his story
of how he'd become friends with Carlos and

Alma didn't ring true. Her instincts had been right on target.

"You are a very beautiful woman, Señorita Jaci. Much too beautiful to spend so much time alone."

He stepped even closer, into her space, and trailed a finger down her arm. Her skin crawled at his touch. "I appreciate the compliment, Enrique, but I really have to go."

"That's too bad. I was hoping we could get to know each other better."

She backed away a step. "Perhaps later."

"If I didn't know better, I'd think you were afraid of me."

"Why would I be?"

He reached over and wrapped his hand around her wrist. He didn't squeeze, but she felt the power in his grip all the same.

"Maybe you are afraid of hot-blooded Hispanic men."

"Maybe." Especially ones who pretended to be someone they weren't.

"Let me take you for a ride in my boat. One night in the moonlight and you will forget this Raoul who follows you around like a puppy dog."

Or she'd end up sinking to the bottom of

the Gulf of Mexico. "There's not supposed to be moonlight tonight. I hear there's a storm brewing."

"There's always my room in the villa. Just the two of us. And a bottle of very good tequila."

"Sorry, I'm really busy this afternoon and tonight."

"Then it is my loss. I'm leaving early in the morning."

He let go of her arm, and she wasted no time in getting out of there.

She was certain Carlos knew Enrique's true identity, but just as sure Raoul didn't, and she couldn't wait to fill him in.

He was waiting on the dock when she stepped into the clearing. "Where in the devil did you disappear to?" he demanded. "I told you I didn't want you going off by yourself."

"I was only standing in the shade, reading a very interesting report I got back from the lab."

"Good news?"

"Surprising news. I'll tell you all about it when we get back to the pool house."

"No way." He grabbed her arm. "I hate those waiting games. What gives?"

"Enrique Lopez isn't Enrique Lopez."

"So who is he?"

"Rodolfo Norberto. Medina Santiago's long-dead brother."

Raoul muttered a curse under his breath. "Are you sure?"

"The fingerprints are a perfect match. Apparently his death was faked to allow him to escape his country after his father was overthrown."

She gave him the rest of the details on the way back to her apartment. He realized the same as she had that Carlos had to know the man's real identify, but Raoul was as confused as she was as to what Enrique's presence on the island meant.

Alma was back at her window when they reached the courtyard. It was weird, but all of a sudden Jaci had the strange feeling that while the Santiago girls were most surely dead, Medina Santiago was alive. And that the woman in the window knew where she was.

RAOUL TWISTED IN THE SHEETS AND tried to get comfortable on the lumpiest mattress he'd ever endured. But even if he'd been cradled in a featherbed, he doubted he'd be asleep, not with the wind and rain battering the windows. Or with the even more troublesome storm shaking his insides to the core.

He'd come here to talk his great-uncle into getting the medical care that might save his life. Now Raoul was so caught up in Jaci, he could barely think of Carlos or anything else.

Lightning lit the sky like fireworks, and a clap of thunder rattled the windows in the pool house. Raoul wondered if Jaci was asleep, or if was she lying awake as he was, listening to the storm, thinking of him, wanting him the way he wanted her.

And he did want her, wanted to hold her, to kiss her again and again, to feel her body next to his, to... God help him, he wanted to make love with her. He wanted it so badly he could taste it.

He'd had two years of thinking he had no right to feel anything. But whether or not he had the right, he was so hungry for Jaci right now it was all he could do not to barge into her room and sweep her up in his arms.

Another clap of thunder rumbled, even louder than before, followed by pitiful yelping. What the devil? Surely Tamale hadn't gotten left out in the pouring rain.

Raoul went to the window and searched for the dog, catching a quick glimpse of him when lightning zigzagged across the sky. The yelp changed to a howl—a pitiful one, as if he were sick or hurt.

Opening the door, Raoul called to him from the covered loggia. The dog tried to come, but was apparently tangled up in something.

Raoul couldn't just leave him there. He wiggled into his jeans, grabbed his windbreaker and a flashlight, and half ran, half slipped down the wet steps.

It didn't take but a second to find the problem. Tamale had gotten caught up in a piece of metal filigree. His right front paw was stuck in one of the holes, and a twisted extension had become caught on the trunk of one of the palm trees.

"Take it easy, boy. I know it hurts, but give me a second and I'll get you free."

The dog whimpered, but stood perfectly still while Raoul bent the metal and extricated the paw.

Tamale shook, sending a spray of water into Raoul's face. Not that it mattered; he couldn't have been any wetter. He'd planned to take the poor mutt inside with him, but Tamale raced off, obviously heading to his usual port in a storm.

Raoul walked back toward the pool house. Jaci's door was open, and she was standing there in that same yellow nightshirt she'd had on the first night he'd ever seen her.

"Raoul Lazario to the rescue?" she asked, her voice all but drowned out by the wind and rain.

"Something like that."

"Come in and dry off."

His heart slammed against his chest, but as much as he wanted to take her up on that offer, he knew his limitations.

"If I come in, I may not leave."

She didn't answer, just reached out, grabbed his arm and pulled him inside.

Chapter Thirteen

"I'll grab a towel," Jaci said, in a voice that sounded husky even to her own ears. "You strip."

By the time she returned, Raoul's windbreaker was in a wet ball on the tile floor, and streams of water were dripping down his bare chest to disappear beneath the waistband of the partially unzipped jeans.

Raoul stopped unzipping, no doubt aware that she was staring, possibly drooling—so hot for him that she was finding it hard to breathe. There was probably an explanation for her sudden loss of control. She couldn't care less what it was.

She swallowed hard, then stepped in close. She wrapped the towel around his head and rubbed briskly, leaving his thick, dark hair damp and wildly disheveled. He kissed her neck as she moved the towel to his chest to capture the water collecting on the ends of the short, wiry hairs.

It was every inch a man's chest. Muscled. Hard. Gorgeous. She ran her tongue over one nipple, catching a droplet of water.

He moaned, and the thrill of turning him on like that was as heady as her own desire. The towel slipped from her fingers and dropped to the floor. She splayed her hands across Raoul's chest and he fitted his over hers, letting their fingers entwine.

One second they were staring into each other's eyes, the next his arms were around her, his fingers tangled in her hair. And then his mouth found hers.

She melted into the kiss, holding nothing back. She loved the taste of him, the mingling of their breaths, the feel of his tongue tangling with hers. The wetness from his jeans soaked into her nightshirt and right through to her bare skin, a seductive reminder that she was wearing nothing under it.

She wanted Raoul. Wanted every inch of him with a hunger she hadn't known existed. "You're getting me all wet," she whispered, pulling away. "The jeans have got to go."

Her gaze locked on his zipper and his erection pressing hard against the denim. She tried to grasp the tab, but her wet, shaky fingers slipped, brushing against his arousal. She ran her thumbs up and down the denim-clad length of him, loving that he writhed at her touch.

"I'll get the zipper," Raoul whispered, his mouth at her ear, nibbling and sucking her earlobe.

She struggled to help, but it was the first time she'd ever tried peeling wet jeans off a man who had swelled to gigantic proportions. It went much too slowly, but finally the jeans fell, along with every inhibition she'd ever had.

He pulled her against his naked body, and a million new and wanton sensations coursed through her. She held on tight as he kissed her lips, her neck, the soft swell of cleavage.

And then his hands slipped beneath her nightshirt and he cupped both breasts before pushing the wet fabric out of his way and backing her against the wall.

His fingers singed a burning trail up and down her thighs, and she raised her right leg, wrapping it around him so he'd reach higher.

When his fingers finally grazed her most private parts, she buried her lips in the smooth flesh of his shoulder to help hold back her orgasm.

It was no use. She moaned loudly as she filled his hand with a rush of slick wetness that didn't even begin to satisfy. And then he was inside her, filling her and thrusting hard and fast. It was wild and unbridled.

Too passionate. Too hot. Too damn good to last.

He was shaking when the ride was over, his breathing quick and shallow. Her heart was pounding, the pleasure that was trapped inside her showing no signs of letting up.

When her heart slowed enough that she could manage to speak, she looked up and met his smoky gaze. "Is that the best you can do?" she teased, not daring to go anywhere serious in the state she was in.

"No, that was just for starters."

He kissed her again, this time slowly and sweetly and her legs seemed to dissolve beneath her. She wasn't sure exactly what had happened between them except that they'd made love with more passion and raw hunger than she'd ever experienced.

Maybe it was the timing, coming on the heels of all she'd been through the last few days. Maybe it was the isolation and the haunting aura of Cape Diablo. Maybe it was...

No. She wouldn't deal with the *L* word. It was enough that the lovemaking had been perfect in every way. It was too soon to try and make it anything more.

Still, she was filled with a new sweet yearning when Raoul swooped her into his arms and carried her to her bed. The secluded, haunted island had never felt as safe as it did that night in the storm.

JACI WOKE WITH A START IN the middle of the night, instantly sensing that she was not alone. And then she heard Raoul's rhythmic breathing and felt the tenderness between her thighs. It all came back to her in a heated rush, and impulsively she slid a hand between her legs.

She was reacting like a schoolgirl, as if it had been her very first time with a man. It wasn't. She'd made love before. She'd just never made love the way she had last night.

And it hadn't been just a one-time thrill.

They'd brought each other to orgasm three times before Raoul had finally fallen asleep in her bed. Each time had been amazing. Each time the foreplay had been different. Each time had been nothing short of fantastic.

Raoul moved in his sleep and started to mumble something about a collapse and air and...

Allison.

The name was mumbled, but clear enough that there was no mistaking it. Jaci's heart plunged, and the warmth that had coursed through her body a few seconds earlier turned frigid.

She had no right to feel hurt. Raoul hadn't pushed himself on her or made any declarations of affection. He'd given her what she wanted, what she'd needed. They'd made love on a stormy night. It was as simple as that.

Besides, what had she expected from a man who still had his fiancée's picture in a prominent place more than two years after her death?

Still, traitorous tears burned at the back of Jaci's eyelids. Twenty-four years old and she'd finally found the magic people always talked about. Ironically, she'd found it with a man who was still emotionally tied to someone else.

Who'd have thought it could feel so right—yet be so wrong?

RAOUL PULLED ON HIS OLD gray sweatshirt and walked into the courtyard. The sun was brilliant, the air brisk and twenty degrees cooler than it had been before the cold front came blowing in on the heels of the storm.

The temperature, however, was not nearly as chilling as Jaci's mood.

She'd been up and dressed before he woke, and had pulled away when he'd tried to coax her back into bed with him. Obviously she was having serious second thoughts about having been with him.

He didn't blame her. He'd come on too strong, especially the first time. He'd forgotten tenderness, just came at her like a sexstarved maniac.

In a way he had been, but last night wasn't just about sex. It was about Jaci, and the attraction that had been building since the first moment he'd met her. He should have told her that, but then what?

He didn't know if he could handle an intimate relationship no matter how much he wanted to. The guilt pushed so hard that sometimes he didn't want to move on, couldn't convince himself that he deserved love and happiness when Allison didn't even have a life.

Only he was still alive. So where the hell did that leave him?

This was getting him nowhere. He walked over and picked up the piece of metal he'd untangled from Tamale's paw last night. A strange looking contraption, it was almost a foot long and about six inches wide, with some kind of scrolled design. Part of it looked like a Q, but the tail of the letter was twisted into a sharp, jagged edge.

Raoul held it at one angle, then another, trying to get some sense of what it had been. Whatever, it was of no use now.

He started to walk over and toss it in the trash can, then hesitated when he heard Jaci's door open, and saw her step out into the courtyard.

"Can I talk to you a minute?"

"Sure," he answered, knowing from the look on her face this wasn't something he wanted to hear.

She stopped a good foot away from him and kept her gaze downward. "It's about last night."

"What about it?"

"I was… We were…"

"Yeah, we were and we did. I must have done it all wrong if you can't even look me in the eye."

"No, it's not that. You were great." Finally she met his gaze. He could have drowned in the emerald depths of her eyes, but he couldn't read them.

"I was great, but—"

"It's just that, considering the circumstances, I think we should forget last night happened."

"What circumstances would those be?"

She looked away again. "We're just not in the same place. I still want us to—" She switched directions midsentence. "Where did you get that?" She put out her hand and ran a finger over the piece of metal he was holding.

"It's what brought me out in the rain last night. Tamale's right front paw was caught in here," Raoul said, running his fingers around the narrow opening. "And this piece was looped around the trunk of the palm tree nearest the gate."

"Let me see that."

"Okay, but careful, it's got some sharp edges."

She held the metal in front of her, running her fingers over the indentations. "Do you know what this is?"

"Some kind of design, I guess. Seems like it might be part of a word. Look, we don't have to stand here and make conversation."

"I'm not making conversation. I'm telling you that came off the side of Andres Santiago's boat."

"What boat?"

"The one he kept for his personal use. The one that disappeared the same night he and his family did. See, there's the *q* and the *u*. And this bent piece was part of the *t*. The rest is missing, but the name of his boat was *Conquiste*."

Conquer. That made sense. Raoul studied the scrap of metal again. "Are you sure?"

"Pretty sure," she said. "There's a picture in the villa of Andres, Medina, Pilar and Reyna standing beside his boat. Even in the photo I could tell the nameplate was a filigreelike metal and not paint." Her voice rose in excitement. "Do you realize what a breakthrough this might be?"

Actually, he was way ahead of her, but didn't care to steal her thunder. "Why don't you tell me?"

"If this is off Andres's boat, then the yacht must have been sunk that night, so Andres couldn't have used it to escape with his family. That makes it a lot more likely they all met with foul play."

And if part of the vessel had washed up on the island after all this time, the boat was likely in one of the channels that wound between the islands, and not the wide-open waters of the gulf.

Raoul figured Jaci was thinking the same thing or would be soon. There were plenty of places deep enough for a boat to disappear and never be found unless a search crew knew where to look. It definitely wouldn't be the first time surfacing objects had helped locate a sunken boat.

Objects and bones. Like the one Tamale had found the other night, the one Carlos had been so quick to get rid of.

But if Carlos knew that the boat had sunk, then he knew a lot more than he'd ever admitted, the way he'd known but never said that Enrique was Medina's brother.

"Do you still want to talk?" Raoul asked, his mind treading in a mire of dread.

Jaci fingered the piece of metal. "About the boat or about last night?"

"About last night."

"I just hope we can still be friends."

"Sure. Friends. I will delete last night from my hard drive." That was a lie, of course. There was no way in heaven or hell he'd forget making love with Jaci. And no way his hard drive would, either.

But for now he knew what he had to do, and he couldn't wait to get started.

CARLOS KICKED THROUGH THE damp sand, his path lit by moonlight, his ears filled with the sound of breaking waves. Cape Diablo. The beloved island of Andres Santiago. All the makings of paradise. All the horrors of hell.

Andres Santiago had dreamed big and gone after his dreams with a passion that knew no bounds. Smuggling. Illegal arms. Drug trafficking. They were merely the means to finance the dreams. He'd recognized no law but his own, fought only for what he'd believed in.

And he, like Carlos, had believed in General Noberto. Andres had poured much of his fortune into supplying arms to help keep the benevolent dictator in power. Carlos had nothing to give to the cause but himself.

Nothing to give up for the general but the only woman he'd ever loved.

Tears wet Carlos's eyes as the memories took over. He let them flow. He would have never cried back then. Tears were for little boys and old men.

The sound of the waves melded into booming gunfire. The battle was raging. Carlos could hear the blood pounding in his head when the general gave the order to charge. It was all or nothing. Win or die.

The bullet that took Noberto out came from close range, probably shot by one of the general's own men, though Carlos was glad he never knew which of his *camaradas* had been the traitor.

"Go to them, Carlos. Find Maria and Medina and keep them safe. I pass them into your care, my dear, dear friend."

The enemy was already inside the general's villa when Carlos arrived. He'd sneaked past them, praying with every heartbeat that he would be in time. He'd found Maria, shot and dying on the cold, damp floor of the secret passage where she'd run to escape. He cradled her in his arms and put his ear to her lips so that he could hear her final whispers.

"Tell me we did the right thing, Carlos. Tell me the sacrifice was worth it."

"You were his wife, Maria. I was his friend." That might not have been the answer she wanted, but it was all Carlos knew of the truth.

"Find Medina, Carlos. Stay with her and keep her safe. Please don't leave my little girl all alone."

"I promise, *mi querida,* I promise, my love."

Carlos shook loose the memories and focused on the lights of a distant boat. He'd made a mess of his life, failed the people he'd cared about most.

He wouldn't fail this time. He'd finish what he had to do and this time he'd do it right. One last task. Two more graves.

And then it would all be over.

JACI WOKE FROM A SOUND SLEEP to a room that was eerily quiet and pitch-dark. It took a few seconds for her sleep-drugged mind to realize what was wrong.

The generator was out. She'd become so used to the monotonous drone that its absence seemed deafening. The lack of a generator also explained the absolute darkness. Normally, even on moonless nights, dim light from the courtyard filtered through the gauzy white curtains.

Apparently this was a moonless night. It hadn't been overcast earlier, but Jaci knew how quickly that could change in this part of the gulf. Storms constantly formed and dissipated over the water, so that a thunderhead could develop in a matter of minutes.

It wasn't storming tonight. Probably a cover of low clouds was making the island so dark that even now, as her pupils started to adjust, she couldn't see the hand she lifted in front of her face.

She wondered if Carlos had turned off the generator for some reason or if he'd simply forgotten to refuel it.

She rolled over to check the time, realizing as she did that without electricity not only would the time be wrong, but the lighted dial would be as dark as the rest of the room.

But there was no reason to panic. She had a flashlight right next to the bed. And if she needed him, Raoul was just upstairs.

If she needed him...

She didn't. She'd told herself that all afternoon. He was a neat guy, bossy, but more sensitive then he wanted anyone to know. He'd definitely been there for her in Everglades City, and might have saved her life the other day in the villa. Even now he'd disrupted his personal plans to make sure she was safe.

So give him sensitive and thoughtful. And not boring. So totally not boring. And sex with him had been—well, on a scale of one to ten, she'd give it a hundred.

But, bottom line, his heart was already taken.

She'd deal with it. That was for the best. Cape Diablo consumed her life now, but once the project was completed, she'd move on. She'd graduate and start her career. She'd be glad she didn't have him in her life.

She closed her eyes, blinking back tears. Who was she kidding? She'd miss Raoul. She missed him already. But the fact that he hadn't really protested when she'd said they should forget last night was proof enough that he wasn't ready to move past Allison. Even if he'd wanted to, Jaci wasn't sure he could.

She rolled over and caught the scent of him on the pillow next to hers. Grabbing it, she punched it hard, then pulled it into her arms and cuddled it against her chest.

She had to get Raoul off her mind or she'd never go back to sleep. Her eyes were open now, but the blackness closed in on her. It was overwhelming, like the curse of Cape Diablo with its history of violence.

Jaci shivered and pulled the light blanket up to her neck. She was wide-awake, but the impressions taking over her consciousness were more nightmarish than real.

A boy floating in the pool, his face grotesquely misshapen. Pilar Santiago holding a doll that dripped with blood. Alma Garcia dancing in the moonlight with an imaginary partner in a dress that was yellowed and frayed. The name from Santiago's boat washing up on the island from its watery grave.

The authentic and the imagined were equally surreal.

What had really happened on this island? What had Alma and Carlos seen? What had they done?

What had caused the island to take them prisoner? Or was the crumbling, moldy villa itself the source of the evil? Had Wilma St. Clair been painting that evil when she'd turned the flowers creeping across the decaying walls to blood?

This was crazy. Jaci had to stop letting the island's isolation and sinister aura get to her.

Light would help. A quick beam of light so that she could at least see her hand when she put it in front of her face.

She turned and reached for the flashlight. Her hand raked across the small table. Her fingers slid over the alarm clock, then bounced against—someone else's hand.

Jaci jerked away as her heart slammed against her chest. Someone was here in the blackness with her. Someone was standing over her bed.

Chapter Fourteen

Jaci lay perfectly still, paralyzed by fear, sensing the man's presence in the total blackness the way you know when someone is watching you. She listened for his breathing, but it was masked by the pounding of her heart.

Raoul was just upstairs. All she had to do was yell. Even if he was sound asleep, he would hear her and come bursting in to save her. That was Raoul.

But would he come rushing headfirst into a bullet? She couldn't take that chance.

"Who are you?"

There was no answer. The intruder was playing a game with her, a sadistically sick game. If he was there at all.

Could she have imagined the hand resting on the bedside table the way she had the grossly distended body in the pool? The way she'd seen a bloody Pilar and even heard her voice?

Jaci took a deep breath, but the sense of terror intensified. She couldn't just lie here and wait. She had to make a break for it.

She started to roll to the far side of the bed, but the man was quicker. His fingers raked her arm, they locked around her wrist, jerking her back toward the center of the bed.

His other hand covered her face, then stopped at her throat. Something sharp pierced the flesh, and she felt a hot trickle of blood roll to the back of her neck.

"Don't make a sound," he whispered. "If you do, I'll gut you like a hog, the same way I'll do that gringo upstairs if he comes rushing down to save you."

Enrique.

She was sure of it, even though she'd heard his voice only a few times. If he'd ever left the island, he was back.

"What do you want with me?"

"I told you we should get to know each other better. I never like to kill a woman before I've had her."

The mattress sagged as he dropped to the

bed beside her. Her stomach rolled sickeningly. He was going to rape her. His hands and his body would be all over her. And then he'd kill her. It had been his plan all along.

But why? Why would he need her dead? She was no threat to him—unless he was involved in the Santiago mystery?

That was it. He'd killed them. Murdered not just Andres, but his own sister and two innocent little girls. Killed them and somehow gotten his hands on Andres's fortune. That would explain the fancy yacht. But why would he have ever come back to Cape Diablo, much less visited on a regular basis as he'd claimed?

She no longer felt the cold threat of the blade at her neck. Instead she felt Enrique's hands groping her. She retched as her terror fused with revulsion.

Random rules of self-defense chased though her mind.

Use the strongest part of your body. Go for the eyes with your fingers to temporarily blind the enemy. Or for the crotch to buy time for an escape.

And do it with all the strength she could muster in a room so black she couldn't even see her target. Do it even if it meant the knife would plunge into her chest or slice her jugular vein. He had no intention of letting her out of this alive.

Enrique ripped at her panties.

Jaci exploded in repulsion. She swung her free hand and jabbed it into his face. One finger caught his eyeball, and he jerked away, sputtering a stream of vile Spanish curses.

She vaulted to the floor and took off running toward the door that opened into the narrow hallway.

Her right foot slammed into the door frame, crushing her toes against the heavy wood. The pain was horrendous, but she didn't slow down—not until she cleared the hall and ran smack into one of the wicker chairs in the sitting room.

She went over it headfirst, falling into a small table and sending the lamp and everything else on it crashing to the floor around her head.

The racket telegraphed her position, and a second later Enrique grabbed a handful of her hair and jerked her to her feet. But not before she got her fingers around the scrap of jagged metal that had fallen from the toppling table.

She swiped the metal in Enrique's direction. A new stream of filthy vulgarities flew from his mouth, and he shoved her hard, slamming her body against the wall.

Staggering, Jaci blinked, trying to see in a sudden blast of light that blinded her almost as much as the darkness had. But through the glare, she could see Raoul.

"Watch out for Enrique," she yelled, as she jumped over the broken lamp and dashed to the open French doors.

Raoul caught her as she reached the courtyard, and shoved her behind him with the hand holding the flashlight. That's when she saw the gun in his other hand, aimed into the apartment.

Enrique was nowhere in sight.

Jaci rested her head beneath Raoul's shoulder blades.

"Are you okay?" he asked.

"No, but you should see the other guy."

Raoul didn't buy her feeble attempt to fight the terror that still bucked around inside her.

"Did he…?"

"No," she assured him. "I'm fine."

Jaci couldn't see a thing outside the beam

of Raoul's flashlight, but she heard footsteps running away from her apartment. Evidently Enrique had escaped through the bedroom window.

"Stay here," Raoul ordered.

He took off running, the beam from his flashlight dancing across a trail of Enrique's blood. Ignoring Raoul's command, Jaci tried to follow, but lost him in the dark when he cut through the overgrown garden and rounded the villa's north wing.

Panic swelled inside her. Raoul had a gun, but Enrique might have one as well. This was all her fault. She'd refused to listen to Detective Linsky when he'd told her the island was too dangerous. But now it was Raoul, not her, who was facing a killer.

She fell against the vines that climbed the villa, and willed time to go by, while horrifying images from thirty years ago collided with fears of what might be happening to Raoul right now.

A cool mist began to fall. She shivered and wrapped her arms about her chest, keenly aware that she was wearing only a thin, cotton nightshirt that had been touched by Enrique's repulsive hands.

An eternity later, she heard the thud of footsteps and saw Raoul coming toward her, the beam of his light bouncing off the wall and casting him in an eerie glow.

She ran to him, and he took her in his arms and held her so tightly she had to gasp for air.

"I lost him near the swamp," Raoul explained. "I would have gone in after him, but I was afraid he'd doubled back to the pool house."

"Bull said there are muddy bogs in there that can suck you into them and bury you like quicksand."

"Great. Maybe Enrique or Rodolfo, or whatever he calls himself, will be sucking mud before I find him."

She pulled away. "Don't even think of going in there after him. I mean it, Raoul. He's dangerous, and you're not a cop."

He ran the beam of his light up and down her body. "Are you sure you're not hurt?"

"A little banged up from knocking into furniture," she admitted. "I'll live."

"Don't joke about that." He rocked her in his arms, and she heard the pounding of his heart and felt the tension in his muscles.

"Promise me you won't leave me again to

go stalking through the swamp after that monster."

"If he gets away—"

"No. Promise me, Raoul. I mean it. Stay with me. I need you here." She needed him safe.

"Why trust me? I already let you down."

"You saved my life."

"I should have been inside the apartment with you, not sleeping upstairs. But you didn't do too badly at defending yourself. Enrique was bleeding, though not enough that I could find his trail once I lost it."

"I slashed at him with the piece of metal from Andres's boat. Unlike you, it was the only weapon I had. Where did you get that gun?"

"I brought it with me from the boat. Always good to have one out in the gulf. You never know what kind of snakes you might run across."

"Enrique is lower than a rattlesnake."

"You're sure he didn't touch you? He didn't…"

"He didn't rape me," she said, "but he would have."

"And I would have killed him with my bare hands, or died trying."

She had no doubt Raoul meant that. She couldn't define it or even describe it, but there was something between them. A connection that didn't come along every day— maybe not in every lifetime.

Yet it was Allison who haunted his dreams.

JACI TRIED BUT COULDN'T MAKE herself spend the night in the apartment. Enrique's blood was smeared across the floor and the over-turned chair. But it was the fear and revulsion that seemed embedded in the very walls that bothered her most. She would have slept on the floor of Raoul's second-floor space if it had come to that.

But as usual, Raoul came through for her. He'd suggested she grab a few necessities and that they both spend the remainder of the night on his boat. Not only would the beds be ten times more comfortable, but the two of them would have the benefit of his generator. Not to mention his first aid supplies. Jaci had grabbed a change of clothes and a toothbrush in record time.

Right now she was sitting on his sofa with her leg stretched across a padded ottoman. Raoul was busily cleaning her skinned knee.

The lights on the boat made them an easy target if Enrique had wanted to come back for her. She didn't expect that he would. He'd run too fast when Raoul had appeared. It was clear the man liked having the odds stacked in his favor. They wouldn't be now. Raoul's gun was still within reach.

"Your calf is already turning black-and-blue," Raoul said. "So is your left wrist. I'm not sure how you got so banged up in one fall."

"I was moving at the speed of light."

"This knee looks more like you were skidding through gravel."

"Try a floor of broken and cracked tiles."

"How long since you've had a tetanus booster?"

"Just last year."

"Good," Raoul said. "The wounds are mostly superficial, but the skin is broken in a few places and I hate to even think what kind of bacteria thrives in that old pool house."

"Thanks for sharing that with me."

"Sorry, but facts are facts." He twisted the cap from a small bottle of peroxide.

She sucked in her bottom lip while he

doused the cuts, letting the excess soak into the folded towel beneath her knee.

He set the peroxide aside and chose a white tube from the first aid kit. "This might burn, too."

"Now what?"

"Antiseptic." He squirted on a heavy coat of the cream, smoothing it with a sterilized pad. "That about does it for the wounds. How about a hot toddy to help you relax and get a little sleep before sunup?"

"No, thanks, but I could use a hot shower. I feel dirty everywhere he touched me."

Raoul's muscles tightened. "I wish I'd killed him. I wish I'd—"

"It's okay, Raoul, really. I just need a shower. I'll try not to wash all the antiseptic off the knee."

"Don't worry. There's plenty more. While you shower, I'll call the police in Everglades City and tell them about the foiled attack."

"Linsky will say it serves me right for not following his advice."

"Not likely Linsky will be taking calls in the middle of the night."

Jaci swung her leg from the ottoman and slipped her foot back into her sandal. "True, but I'm sure we'll hear from him first thing in the morning. Carlos isn't going to like your calling the police back out here."

"He's got bigger issues than that to deal with."

The comment surprised her. "Like what?"

"Guess there's no reason not to tell you." Raoul dropped to the couch beside her. "Carlos has cancer."

That explained a few things. "So it wasn't fishing that brought you to Cape Diablo?"

"No, I came to try and convince him to leave this godforsaken island. I want him to move in with me in Naples for a while so that he can get the treatment he needs."

"Surely, he's going to."

"You'd think. He doesn't see it that way. I wouldn't have even known about his condition if his oncologist hadn't called me."

Raoul massaged the back of his neck, and suddenly Jaci realized just how much stress he was under.

"Where's the malignancy?"

"In his stomach. He went in thinking he had an ulcer. When tests confirmed cancer, one of the staff specialists, Dr. Young, called Carlos in to explain the diagnosis and recommend treatment. Carlos walked out of his office before he finished, and never went back."

"What is the recommended treatment?"

"Radiation therapy to try and shrink the cancer. If it responds appropriately, they'll operate to remove the tumor and, unfortunately, much of his stomach."

"And the prognosis?"

"He has a forty percent chance of coming out of this okay with aggressive treatment. Six months to a year to live if he does nothing."

"I'm so sorry, Raoul." But more than sorry, she felt partly responsible for Carlos's refusal to accept Raoul's help. "I'm sure my causing a breach between the two of you didn't help your case."

"I don't think it mattered. This is about Alma and that demonic hold she has on him. I'd like to know what really happened thirty years ago in the boathouse, just to see if it explains their bizarre relationship."

"I keep thinking about Enrique's involvement in all of this," Jaci said. "After his actions tonight, I think there's a good chance he killed all four of the Santiagos."

"Sounds feasible to me," Raoul agreed.

"They may have come home and caught him about to make off with the money Andres was said to have lying around the island."

"The legendary missing fortune."

"Exactly. If they found him in the boat-house," Raoul continued, "it would explain the blood."

"But the splatters indicate only two people were shot there. And then there's Pilar. She was—" Jaci caught herself before she said more. "I think I'll take that shower now."

She started to stand, but Raoul grasped her hand and tugged her back down beside him. "What about Pilar?"

"Nothing."

Nothing except that she'd appeared in a bizarre image, lying in a pool of blood, her doll cradled against her small, heaving chest.

Run, Jaci. Run or the wicked witch will kill you, too.

"You're trembling," Raoul said.

"I'm fine," she insisted, knowing she was anything but.

The rational side of her knew that neither Cape Diablo nor the villa could be haunted. Murdered children couldn't reach out to her, not from their deathbed or from the murky pool.

Murdered children. The revelation hit with staggering force. "Andres's son didn't just drown. He was murdered."

"How did you come to that conclusion?"

Jaci didn't realize she'd spoken aloud until she heard Raoul's surprised reaction.

"It's just a hunch," she said. But a powerful one. Enrique might have been in on the crimes, but he wasn't the only one. Alma was involved as well. Alma, the wicked witch.

She must have drowned Andres's son and then gone mad—or more likely she'd been unbalanced all along. Then, somehow, she'd fallen in league with Enrique, perhaps helped him locate the treasure, and been in on the plans to kill the family. Carlos may have been in on the scheme as well.

Only why would Carlos have turned against Andres and General Norberto's daughter?

This time Raoul stood up. He took her hand and tugged Jaci to her feet. "You should have that shower now if you're going to get any more sleep tonight. If you need me, call. I won't be more than a few steps away."

She met his gaze, and felt its warmth wash over her. Not the sensual onslaught she'd felt last night. Her nerves and emotions were far too shot for that after what she'd been through with Enrique. But it felt incredibly safe just to be with Raoul.

"I'll turn down the covers in the big bedroom and leave the antiseptic cream handy. Soap's in the shower. Shampoo, too. And there's toothpaste in the cabinet over the sink."

"Did anyone ever tell you you're a terrific guy?"

He didn't respond.

Because, of course, someone had. The fiancée whose pictures still claimed the most prominent spot on his boat. Dead for two years, but still in his life—and in his dreams. Jaci turned to stare at the photographs.

Raoul stepped between her and the pictures, as if reading her mind. "You must know I care for you, Jaci, but it's just…"

"Just that you're still in love with Allison," she said, finishing his sentence for him when it didn't seem that he could.

"That's not what I was going to say."

"You called her name in your sleep after we made love."

"I loved Allison. I'm not denying that, but…" He took a deep breath and exhaled slowly. "I killed Allison, Jaci. I killed her as surely as if I'd put a bullet in her head."

"What are you saying?"

"She didn't want me to take the crew on the dive that day, said she had a bad feeling about it. I blew off her concerns."

"So you didn't back out?"

"No, four of us prepared for the dive, and at the last minute, Allison decided to join us."

Raoul's voice dropped, and Jaci felt as if he were moving away from her, though he hadn't taken a step.

"The other three crew members took the back of the sunken sailing vessel. Allison and I took the front. It was a preliminary exploration, just to determine the condition of the ship and its contents. Gung ho, as always, I rushed ahead of her. I didn't see her when I looked back, and thought her apprehension had gotten the better of her and she'd decided to surface."

"But she hadn't?"

"No. The plan was that we stay together, but something down a side corridor must have grabbed her attention or else she thought I'd turned that way. A few minutes later, the hull of the ship shifted and part of a wall caved in. She was crushed. By the time we got her to the surface, she was dead."

Jaci felt his grief and, to an extent, she even understood his guilt. She ached to wrap her arms around him, but it seemed as if he'd moved into another world, one where she didn't belong.

"If I'd called off the dive, or even if I'd gone back to check on Allison when I didn't see her behind me, she'd be alive today."

Or he might have been in the same corridor and died with her. "It's done, Raoul. You can't undo it. You have to let it go."

"Do you think I haven't told myself that same thing a thousand times? I've tried to put it behind me, but then something happens and the guilt bushwhacks me all over again. How can I just move on? What right do I have to happiness or love, when she doesn't even have a life?"

Anguish tore at his voice and deepened

the lines on his face. He was literally ravaged by guilt.

"So where does that leave us, Raoul?"

"I don't have the answers. All I know is that when I'm with you, I feel things again. Not just the sex, though that was incredible. It's like coming home when you thought you never would. The sun is brighter. Laughter comes easier. Even food tastes better." He stepped closer and took her hands in his. "I'm sure I'm saying this all wrong."

He was saying it just fine, but what kind of relationship could they have with him wallowing in guilt and calling Allison's name in his sleep? Jaci's thoughts spun into a whirlwind of confusion.

"I can't deal with this, Raoul. Not tonight."

"I'm not asking for anything but a chance, Jaci. I don't want to lose you."

And she didn't want to lose him. If she wasn't already hopelessly in love with him, she was well on the way. But she'd never be satisfied to come in second to a memory and his overwhelming guilt.

He released her hands slowly, letting his fingertips slide to hers as she pulled away.

Strange, but as she walked away from him, it felt an awful lot as if she'd just said a final goodbye.

"WE HAD ALL OUR SURVEILLANCE ducks in a row and were ready to catch Enrique in the act when you arrived on the island and tossed your little blood-splatter monkey wrench into the works."

Jaci sat in the boat cabin across from Paige and Linsky, trying to assimilate this information along with everything else they had thrown at her and Raoul over the last few minutes.

Amazingly, she'd fallen into a sound sleep after her shower, only to wake at 7:00 a.m. to the drone of helicopters circling the island. Detectives Linsky and Paige had arrived at Cape Diablo an hour later, demanding to know every detail of last night's encounter with Enrique. Like her, they agreed that his actions might well indicate an involvement with the Santiago murders.

However, that was not their primary concern. They'd finally admitted they weren't detectives, nor were they with the Everglades

Police Department, though the local police were cooperating with their operation.

Linsky worked for Homeland Security. Paige was with Border Patrol. They were both part of a special interagency task force trying to stop smuggling of goods, drugs and illegal aliens into the country. Enrique was their number one target.

"Cape Diablo has always been a hotbed of smuggling activity," Linsky explained. "The location is perfect. It has access to hundreds of channels that weave through the mangrove islands and to the open waters of the Gulf."

"And it has that hidden deepwater cove on the southern tip of the island that can accommodate the larger boats while hiding them from view," Paige added.

"I understand the smuggling aspect," Jaci said. "I'm just not clear how my investigation interfered with your plans."

"It started when you contacted Mac Lowell."

"I only wanted to talk about the photos he took of the original crime scene."

Linsky sipped his coffee. "Yes, but when

the local police investigated the murder, they discovered that right after Mac made the call to you, he made another to a cell phone registered to one of the several aliases Enrique uses for doing business in the States."

"Then you already knew his real identity?"

"Yes, but it was a fairly recent discovery and not one that had any real significance to our investigation."

"Why would Mac Lowell call Enrique?"

"We don't have that figured out," Linksy admitted. "Maybe Lowell worked for him and Enrique decided he'd become dispensable."

That wasn't much of an explanation in Jaci's mind. "Wouldn't it be more likely Lowell was paid off thirty years ago to keep quiet about something he'd discovered at the original crime scene, and now that I was calling him about the photos, he was demanding an additional bribe?"

"Could be," Paige admitted.

Linsky uncrossed his legs and leaned in close, directing his intimidating gaze at Jaci. "I'm not putting you down, Miss Matlock. Your professor says you're top of the class, and I can see why. But if you're not off Cape

Diablo by nightfall, I'll have no choice but to arrest you."

"On what grounds?"

"That you're interfering with official law enforcement activities."

She'd love to leave Cape Diablo. She'd never been anywhere that reeked of evil and violence the way this island did. But Linsky, Paige and their interagency task force were only interested in getting Enrique. If she just walked away, who would ever find out the truth about what had happened to Pilar and Reyna? Who would ever know if the evil witch had drowned the little boy in the pool?

Paige turned his attention to Raoul. "I'd suggest you leave the island as well. If Enrique returns to the area, he won't hesitate to kill you for getting in his way last night."

Raoul walked over and stood behind Jaci, facing both men. "What makes you think Enrique's left the area?"

"We've had helicopters in the air all morning searching for his boat. It's not docked anywhere on Cape Diablo and hasn't been spotted in the vicinity."

"A crew member could have taken the boat

off the island and left Enrique behind," Raoul reminded him.

"I assure you if Enrique's on the island, we'll find him."

"Then you plan to search the swamp and the villa?"

"If we find evidence he's still here. But take my word for it. That's very unlikely. He's not going to let himself get trapped on an island with no way off."

"I agree," Raoul said, "unless he has un-finished business here."

"More reason why you and Miss Matlock should go back to the mainland."

"Guess that covers everything," Paige said, standing up. "Except I'll have to ask you to stay out of your apartment, Miss Matlock, until we and the CSI team are through in there. We need samples of Enrique's DNA to match with bits of skin found under Mac's fingernails. After that, you'd be wise to pack your things and get out, the sooner the better."

Raoul walked over and opened the door, letting in a cold, damp draft that seemed fitting with the mood of the day. "I'd like to know my uncle and Alma Garcia will be protected," he said, "from Enrique and from harassment from government investigators."

"I'll make sure of it," Linsky promised. "And, Miss Matlock, if you want to go to work for Homeland Security, I'll be glad to give you a recommendation. You're smart and stubborn, and don't give up when the game gets rough, just the kind of person our country needs in its law enforcement ranks."

"Thanks," Jaci said. "I'll give that some thought." But it wasn't on her mind as she picked up the empty coffee cups to take them to the sink. She paused as she passed the bookcase. The pictures of Alison were conspicuously absent.

Once Linsky and Paige were off the boat, Raoul joined Jaci in the kitchen. "I can take you to the mainland whenever you're ready. You are going back today, aren't you?"

"I don't seem to have a lot of choice."

He took her hands in his. "I can't say I'm sorry to hear that."

"What about you, Raoul? What will you do about Carlos?"

"I'll try again to talk some sense into him, but I'm going back to work as well. I have the *Conquiste* to locate and explore.

Actually, I need to go and make some phone calls now. There are still a few crew members I haven't been able to reach, and I need to arrange for supplies and getting my diving boat outfitted for the search."

Only instead of leaving, he stood there, still holding her hands long after the silence between them grew awkward. Going back to the mainland would not only mean giving up on finding the truth about what had happened to Pilar and Reyna, it would mean not seeing Raoul every day. It might mean not seeing him at all.

His phone rang, and he dropped her hands and he went to answer it. She poured herself another cup of coffee, then grabbed a pad and pen and went out to the deck.

Carlos was mending fish nets at the end of the dock. He looked up once and stared menacingly at her as a helicopter flew directly overhead. She smiled and waved. He ignored her, and she went back to her notes, painfully aware that almost every scenario she came up with for the night of the murders had him playing a role.

It was a good thirty minutes later when she heard a loud thud. She looked up to see

Carlos stretched out on the deck, holding his stomach and writhing in pain.

She yelled for Raoul as she ran to Carlos. By the time she got to him, his eyes were rolling back in his head and he was shaking uncontrollably. She put a hand on his wrist to check his pulse. It was dangerously slow.

"You've got to get him to the hospital," she said.

Only there was a problem. Linsky and Paige's boat had the *Quest* blocked so that it couldn't clear the dock.

"You get Carlos on board," Jaci called. "I'll move the other boat." She jumped on deck, but realized as soon as she got to the helm that one of the men had removed the key.

She yelled that to Raoul and took off at a dead run to find someone to move the boat. Sand flew behind her as she raced toward the pool house, sure she'd find the CSI team still combing her apartment.

She was wrong. The pool house was empty. Apparently, they'd started their investigation somewhere else. Panicked, she ran back to the courtyard. Alma was standing in the weed-choked jungle of a garden, shoveling dirt and tossing it onto the brick path near the north wing of the villa.

Jaci raced toward her, hoping she could make her understand. "I'm looking for some men, Alma. Not tenants, just visitors. Have you seen them?"

She didn't look up, but dug all the faster.

"Carlos is sick, Alma. He's very sick and Raoul needs to take him to the hospital. If you've seen the men, tell me where they are."

Alma didn't respond, and there was no time to waste trying to get through to her. Jaci turned her back on the woman, and yelled for help.

And that's when the cold, hard face of the shovel slammed into the back of her head. Jaci's knees buckled, and she went down into the jungle of weeds. The last thing she saw before she passed out was the twisted face of the evil witch.

Run, Jaci, run.

But now it was too late.

Chapter Fifteen

Jaci opened her eyes. The room was a blur of colors and translucent shapes. She tried to move, but her head seemed to weigh a ton. Even swallowing was difficult, and she felt as if she were in a hospital—or funeral home—choking on the sickeningly sweet scent of gardenias.

She blinked repeatedly, and slowly the colors and swirling shapes began to coalesce into recognizable forms. She was lying atop a white chenille spread in the middle of a wide bed. Dozens of lit candles, assorted sizes, all of them white, lined the bedside table and heavy wooden mantel.

The glow from the candles cast shadows on the massive Spanish armoire and the hanging statues of saints that dominated the wall in front of her. And amid all the smoke and glittering candlelight, there was photograph after photograph of Andres Santiago.

This wasn't a bedroom, but a memorial—an incredibly creepy shrine. The haze in Jaci's mind continued to clear.

She remembered Carlos rolling around the deck in pain, remembered running to find Linsky and Paige, remembered the blow to her head. And now she was where she'd wanted to be ever since she'd arrived on Cape Diablo.

She was on the third floor of the villa. She'd entered Alma Garcia's world—a world where the dead and the living coexisted and time stood still.

But this was not the way Jaci had hoped to see it. Her right arm began to cramp. She tried to pull it from beneath her, but her wrists scraped against the scratchy cords of rope that bound them. She couldn't actually see her ankles, but could tell her they were tied as well.

Someone started humming, and Jaci twisted until she caught sight of Alma, standing near a window that looked out over the beach and white-capped waters of the gulf. She was in the familiar, tattered white dress, cradling a baby doll in one arm.

The doll looked a lot like the one Tamale

had found on the beach, except this one wasn't ravaged by saltwater. Alma's other hand held a small black pistol.

She seemed oblivious of Jaci being in the room, though she must have dragged her here and tied her up. Only carrying Jaci up three flights of very steep stairs would be quite a feat for a frail woman like Alma.

She would have had to have help. Jaci shuddered as the obvious explanation filled her with a new wave of dread.

Alma hadn't carried her up the stairs. Enrique had.

There was no sign of the man, but Jaci was sure he hadn't gone far. Perhaps to bolt the doors so that Raoul couldn't come bounding to her rescue. Or maybe he'd gone to kill Raoul, saving her to last.

No. She couldn't start thinking like that. If she did, she'd never escape. She had to stay in control and find a way to get through to Alma before Enrique returned.

"Hello, Alma."

Alma stepped toward the bed. "Don't say the name of that lying whore inside this sacred room. Do you hear me? I won't have it!"

Jaci sucked in a shaky breath and tried to make sense of Alma's comment. Was it because she'd killed Andres that she wouldn't let her own name be spoken inside the room she'd made into his shrine? Was this some kind of penance to pay for her sins?

"You must miss Andres," Jaci said, keeping her voice low and steady, and trying to reach Alma on another level.

"Of course I miss him."

"Were you in love with Andres?"

"We loved each other. He belonged to me. So did this dress." Alma lifted a handful of the threadbare fabric, only to let it slip back through her fingers.

Jaci had no idea how much of Alma's delusions were true, but even if they'd all been, there wasn't time for this now. "Carlos is very sick. He needs us," Jaci pleaded. "Untie me so we can help him."

Alma gave no sign of hearing her. Instead she walked to her dressing table and lifted the top of an old-fashioned record player, carefully placing the needle on the turning disk. When the music started, she lay down the gun. And then she wrapped herself in the arms of her invisible lover and started to waltz around the room.

The gun was out of her hands. That was a good sign, but it wasn't enough. "Please untie me, Alma. Andres wants you to free me so I can help his friend Carlos."

Alma waltzed to the bed, then leaned over and cupped one hand around her mouth as if she were a young girl sharing an innocent secret with a friend.

"Reyna and Pilar aren't really in their bedroom. They're dead," she murmured.

"Did you kill them?"

"I had to. I had to make them pay. She stole my dress and was dancing with Andres. I had to make them pay."

"What about Andres's son? Did you drown him in the pool?"

Alma's eyes went wild. "Who told you?"

"I saw him there. He told me himself."

"That was her fault, too. She made him like her more than me. It was all part of her plan to steal Andres away from me."

"You were right to kill her. Carlos was right to help you, but now you have to help him. Untie me. Please, untie me or Carlos will die and you will be left on Cape Diablo all alone."

"No. Carlos can't leave me."

"Then untie me now so we can help him. You must hurry before Enrique comes back."

"Andres wants me to untie you?"

"Yes."

Finally, they were getting somewhere. Alma dropped to the bed beside her. Jaci rolled over to make it easier for her to get to the ropes at her wrist, but instead of working on knots, Alma opened the drawer of the bedside table and pulled out a knife. It was the same one she'd threatened Jaci with on the beach, or else very similar.

Jaci held her breath until the woman had slipped the point of the blade between the strands of rough rope.

"She was only a servant girl," Alma said as she sawed at the tough cord. "She should never have danced with my husband."

Poor woman. She was totally nuts, so delusional she'd confused her identity with that of the woman she'd killed. Either that or—

That was it! The missing piece to the puzzle. The one flaw in every scenario Jaci had come up with. The explanation for Carlos's undying loyalty and for Enrique's visits to the island.

"You're Medina."

CARLOS WAS ON THE BOAT and ready to go. Tamale was as well, standing by his adopted master and licking the gnarled hand that kept sliding off the bed. Raoul felt his uncle's pulse. It was stronger than it had been when he'd first lifted him from the deck.

Raoul's was racing. Jaci should have been back by now. Even with helicopters circling overhead and cops more populous than flies on the island, he shouldn't have let her go off by herself.

"I'll be back, Uncle Carlos. Hang in there."

Carlos only nodded as Raoul hit the deck and jumped to the dock. Linsky and Paige were a few yards away, walking toward the dock, but Jaci was nowhere in sight.

"Where's Jaci?" he called.

"Isn't she with you?"

"No. She went to her apartment to look for you so you could move your boat. Carlos is sick and I have to get him to the hospital at once."

"We haven't seen her," Linksky said, and something in his voice sliced Raoul's heart right in two.

"We weren't in the apartment," Paige said,

"but a couple of the cops have found evidence that Enrique may still be on the island and hiding out in the swamp."

Raoul didn't wait to hear more. Jaci was in trouble or she'd have been back. He had to find her. He could not lose her. He could not fail another woman he loved.

THE DOOR TO THE BEDROOM flew open just as Jaci's hands slid free. She grabbed the knife Medina dropped and rolled back into place, as if her arms were still tied, as Enrique stomped into the room. His clothes were coated in red mud, and the rotting stench of the swamps emitted from him with every move.

"I told you to call me the second she opened her eyes."

"It's okay," Medina explained. "She's one of us now. She understands I had to kill them."

"You crazy bitch. Do you want to spend the rest of your worthless life rotting in some gringo prison?" Enrique shoved Medina from the bed and away from Jaci.

The woman knotted her thin hands in the folds of her dress and slunk to the corner like a little girl who'd been punished. "We have to help Carlos so he won't leave me here alone to look for the treasure."

"You idiot. There's no treasure. There never has been. Your stupid husband wasted it all on this crumbling stucco relic."

"Don't call Andres stupid."

"He was stupid and he slept with whores." Enrique scanned the room. "Where's the gun?"

Medina reached it a heartbeat before he did, only this time she pointed it at Enrique.

"Andres wasn't stupid. He loved me."

"Hand me the gun, Medina."

"No. Let the woman go. If you don't let her go, Carlos will die. I can't stay here by myself. I can't. The villa hates me."

"The villa is nothing but stucco and wood. Now hand me the gun."

"No." She pointed the short barrel right at his head.

"Don't be a dope, Medina. We're home free. Jaci can't prove a thing with her blood splatter theory. Besides, she'll be dead. Now hand me the gun."

Medina turned the gun from Enrique to Jaci.

"Don't do it, Medina," Jaci pleaded, fitting

her hand around the knife. "Don't let him kill me, or we can't save Carlos."

But Medina started to sway the way she had that night on the beach. The gun fell from her hands, and Enrique scooped it up. Jaci hurled the knife at Enrique in one quick motion. She hit her target, but not before he got off the shot.

The pain was white-hot, so excruciating that Jaci had to fight to keep her focus. The knife was lodged in Enrique's chest, but apparently not the heart. He was leaning against the dressing table, struggling to dislodge the blade. The gun was on the floor where he'd dropped it, just inches from his feet. Behind him flames from the overturned candles were licking their way across the lacy runner that covered the heavy wood.

Medina was sobbing and wringing her hands.

Jaci scooted from the bed and onto the floor. She had to get to the gun, but with her ankles still tied, she'd have to move slowly to keep from falling.

Only the room had started to spin, and the floor seemed to be rolling like waves at high tide. She grabbed the wall for support, but her hand slipped in a stream of her own blood, and she fell against the bedside table. Her arms raked across it, knocking one of the photographs of Andres and a half-dozen candles onto the white spread as she sank to the floor.

Reeling from vertigo, Jaci closed her eyes. Just a second. That's all she could spare. When she opened them again, the room was ablaze and a blood-soaked Enrique was standing over her with murder in his eyes.

She looked at the door, half expecting Raoul to come bounding through it. He didn't. There was only Enrique. And Medina—twirling in the midst of the burning room as if she were dancing again with Andres.

Jaci felt the heat of the blaze and smelled the stench of the unspeakable evil that haunted Cape Diablo and this dreaded villa of death.

So she closed her eyes again and thought only of Raoul. She imagined herself safe in his arms. So safe, she didn't even hear the gun when it fired again.

Chapter Sixteen

Curls of smoke were drifting out the third-floor windows of the villa by the time Raoul made it to the courtyard. He spotted the shovel immediately and wasted no time in smashing a window and breaking into the house.

He raced up the three flights of stairs, not daring to think what he might find at the top. He just knew he couldn't be too late. He might deserve it, but not Jaci. Please, God. Not Jaci.

Head down and gun drawn, he followed the smoke to the open door at the end of the hallway. He stepped inside, and for one horrible moment, his heart stopped beating. Jaci was lying facedown in a pool of blood.

He took in the rest of the scene at once. Alma had taken a bullet to the head, and there was no way she was alive. A dazed and bloody Enrique was lying on the floor, covered with blood. A broken statue lay beside him.

Jaci groaned and rolled over, and Raoul's heart all but stopped. She was alive, and that was all he needed to know.

"Are you real?" Jaci whispered. "Or am I dead?"

"I'm real, baby. I'm real, and we're leaving this hellhole of an island together."

He bent to gather her into his arms as flames cracked and crackled around them.

"You can't leave Medina," Jaci said. "She saved my life."

"If you mean Alma, she's dead," Raoul said, knowing that even if she wasn't, there wouldn't be time for him to carry both women out of the burning house.

"She's dead, and you will be, too," Enrique bellowed.

Raoul turned just in time to see the gun in his hand.

But there was no way in this world Raoul was going to lose Jaci to a bullet now. Enraged, he let her slide from his arms, as he charged Enrique head-on. He might die. Jaci wouldn't.

Gunfire shook the room.

Enrique gasped and rolled onto his back.

Raoul spun around as Linsky and Paige stepped through the open door.

"You missed the party," Jaci said.

Linsky just shook his head. "Get her out of here, Raoul, before she destroys the rest of the ten thousand islands."

Raoul was already lifting her into his arms. A half second later, he had her out the door.

JACI WAS STRETCHED OUT ON a cot in the back of the medic helicopter Linsky had called for Carlos while rushing to follow Raoul into the villa.

"How is Carlos?" she asked, thinking as she did that her voice sounded as if it came from about ten feet above her.

"Hanging in there. He's about as out of it as you are, though. How do you feel?"

"Woozy."

"That's from the pain medication in the IV," the paramedic explained. "But you're doing great. Pressure's in the safe zone, and the bleeding's under control. How's that arm feeling?"

"No feeling at all." She looked down to make sure it was still there. "What's the verdict?"

"I wouldn't sign up for any weight lifting competitions in the near future. That bullet ripped through a lot of muscle and tissue just below the shoulder, but it will heal. You're a very lucky woman."

She looked up at Raoul. "Yeah, I am. Very lucky."

"What a sight!" the pilot called over the drone of the engines. "That old house looks like a giant bonfire. But catch it quick, or you'll miss it, 'cause we are out of here."

"Good thing those cops and that guy they had handcuffed made it out of the house when they did," the paramedic said. "Another five minutes, and they'd have been toast."

Jaci tried to sit up, but the second she put weight on her right arm, she was stabbed with agonizing pain.

"Take it easy," Raoul murmured. "We'll be at the hospital soon."

"I have to see it," she whispered. "I have to see the end."

The paramedic started to argue with her,

but Raoul cut him off. "No use to fight her. You can't win. Besides, she earned this one."

He fitted his arms behind her shoulders and lifted her so that she could see the island through the open door of the copter. Jaci stared at the brilliant flames leaping through the clouds of dark smoke.

The monstrous villa was consumed by the raging fire. It was as if the evil had erupted like a volcano, obliterating not only the house but Medina herself, and the delusional world she'd created.

The images that had haunted Jaci on the island hit again, only this time the boy in the pool was smiling and two beautiful little girls with long, black hair were waving to her from the beach.

"Medina's world is over," Jaci said as Raoul lowered her back to the cot.

"Medina?"

Of course, he didn't know yet. There were lots of things she hadn't told him, such as how Medina had hit Enrique with the statue just when he was about to put a second bullet into Jaci. After all the woman had done in her sordid life, she'd been shot and killed by her own brother while trying to save someone else. What kind of twisted fate was that?

But Enrique had still held the gun and wasn't so dazed that he'd have let Jaci escape if Raoul had not come to the rescue.

"Are you getting tired of saving me, Raoul?"

"Yes. So don't do anything else dangerous."

"Did I tell…" Her tongue was getting too thick to tell Raoul what she was thinking. So she just held his hand and drifted off, smiling at how thrilled her mother would be to know that she'd finally found a man she could love.

Epilogue

Four months later

Satisfied that the project summation was just as she wanted it, Jaci typed the last sentence: "Hell hath no fury like a woman scorned."

Medina Norberto Santiago had been proof of that. The crimes on that long-ago night had gone down pretty much as Jaci had concluded. The intricacies of what happened before and after the murders had been filled in by Enrique, who was hoping for a bit of leniency for murdering Mac Lowell and attempting to murder Jaci, and by Carlos, who no longer felt he had to protect Medina at any cost.

Additional evidence, including what remained of the bodies, was discovered when Raoul's ocean salvage operation raised the

Conquiste. It was a convoluted story of infidelity, rage, duplicity and misguided loyalty—motivations as old as time, yet as current as the day's headlines of any major newspaper.

Andres had given all the servants the night off so that they could attend Cinco de Mayo festivities on the mainland with friends and family. They had all taken advantage of that opportunity except Alma, who'd changed her mind about going at the last minute, and never left the island.

Andres, Medina and his daughters had returned to Cape Diablo just after midnight, much to Medina's displeasure. She'd wanted to stay and party until dawn. Andres, however, had business to take care of. He was expecting a major drug shipment to arrive from Central America in the wee hours of the morning, one that he would disburse to major U.S. drug traffickers for a huge profit.

Medina had put the girls to bed and then gone back to the bedroom she shared with Andres, to continue the argument she'd started on the boat. When she couldn't find him in the villa, she'd gone to the old boathouse, thinking he'd be there drinking with his buddy Carlos, who'd returned even earlier than she and Andres.

But it had been the young and innocent Alma she'd spied through the window, wearing one of Medina's white festival dresses and stealing her husband from her just as she'd stolen his children's affections.

He'd pay. They both would.

She flew back to the house in a rage, determined to hurt him the way he'd hurt her. And nothing had ever hurt Andres as much as when she'd drowned his only son.

She suffocated Reyna with a pillow and planned to do the same to Pilar. But the younger girl had awakened and fought back, so Medina had picked up the statue and crushed her skull. Then she'd taken one of Andres's guns and gone to the boathouse.

She burst into the place and fired, killing Alma with the first shot. Andres had rushed her to take the gun away, and it had gone off in the scuffle. He also fell dead. At least that was the story Medina had hysterically related to Enrique and Carlos when they'd arrived at the boathouse searching for Andres so he could oversee the drug exchange.

Enrique was the one who'd come up with the bizarre plan for Medina to claim to be Alma. They were near the same age, both beautiful Hispanic women with long, dark hair. They could make it work as long as the servants didn't return to the island. He'd called on Carlos's loyalty to their father to persuade him to go along with it, never knowing that it was the promise Carlos had made to their dying mother that had sealed the deal.

Enrique took over the drug smuggling in Andres's absence, making himself a very rich man in the process. Medina, having suffered from a severe personality disorder all her life, proceeded to go completely mad with the help of the illegal drugs Enrique provided.

But it was Carlos who'd suffered most of all, Jaci had concluded in her report. He'd given up his life because of a promise he'd made to another man's wife—the only woman Carlos had ever loved. In the end, he'd planned to overdose and kill both himself and Alma with drugs he'd had brought in from Mexico.

Jaci took the report from the printer, clipped it together and slipped it into the folder with copies of pictures of the blood splatters, the villa and the recovered *Conquiste,* plus charts she'd drawn on how the evidence all fit together.

She'd made no mention in her report of the boy whose image she'd seen in the murky pool. Nor had she mentioned her eerie experience in the girls' bedroom, when Pilar had warned her about the wicked witch.

Looking back, Jaci decided it could have all been illusions brought on by the isolation and her own obsession with solving the case. That was the only reasonable explanation.

But she didn't fully buy it. The aura of evil that had clung to Cape Diablo and the crumbling villa was too powerful to be imagined. The children who'd been so cruelly and violently murdered had haunted the island as surely as the waters of the gulf pounded its shores.

At least that's the way Jaci saw it, and who was to say she wasn't right? Except for her professor, if she'd been stupid enough to put that in the report.

With the thesis project complete, things were in order for her to graduate in May—

a few months later than she'd planned, but she'd gone through too much not to finish this project the way she wanted it done. She'd needed a few weeks of healing before she could type. She didn't have to wait to start her career, however. She'd taken a job with the Miami Police Department. Tomorrow was moving day.

Her phone rang. Her heart jumped as she picked it up to check the caller ID. It was only her mom.

"Did you finish that report you were working on?" her mother asked.

"About five minutes ago."

"Are you seeing that diving guy tonight?"

"No, I'm not seeing Raoul." Because he hadn't asked.

"Good, then you have no excuses why you can't go to dinner with Clarence and me tonight. We're meeting the Baxters at seven. Their son, Matthew, is going to be with them. He's single and a surgeon. You probably don't remember, but you met him at Claiborne's Gallery the night you got that idea for that horrid Cape Fear project."

"Cape Diablo."

"Whatever. Anyway, tell me you'll join

us. You shouldn't spend your last night in town alone."

Jaci tried to think of a reason to say no. There really wasn't any. "Okay, Mom, dinner it is."

"That's great. Wear something nice and don't talk about crime all night. You'll never get a man that way."

Maybe her mom was right, Jaci decided, as she wrote down directions for the restaurant.

She was crazy in love with Raoul. And unless she'd misread every sign, he was just as in love with her. He told her so—even when they weren't making love. How often did men do that? They'd spent lots of time together during her recovery. He'd even made great strides toward putting the guilt behind him, and was excited about his career again.

There was just this one small problem. Raoul had yet to say those four little words that Jaci had hoped to hear before she left for Miami. Not only had he not asked her to marry him, he'd never uttered the *M* word.

She showered and put on the sexiest little black dress in her closet. Not that she cared about impressing Matthew the surgeon, but her ego did need a major boost unless she wanted to end up in Pityville tonight.

The doorbell rang just as she brushed on some lip gloss. Probably a lost pizza delivery man. Happened all the time in her apartment complex. She peeked out the peephole, but all she saw was a huge bouquet of flowers.

Disappointment kicked her in the heart. Was this it? Was Raoul chickening out and sending flowers in lieu of a personal good-bye?

The bell rang again, and she finally gave in and opened the door.

"Raoul."

"Of course. You didn't think I'd let you leave for Miami without saying goodbye."

"It crossed my mind."

"I've been busy."

And now he was here, making a party of her leaving, not only bearing flowers but champagne. "What are we celebrating?"

"Your new job. And Carlos." Raoul took two glasses from a white gift bag.

She set the flowers on the bare kitchen table while he uncorked the champagne and filled the glasses.

"What's Carlos's good news?"

"The judge granted him a suspended sentence based on his age, health and cooperation. And the latest MRI shows that treatment has been even more effective than Dr. Young had hoped."

"That's great," she said, trying to get in the mood of the celebration. She was thrilled for Carlos, but that didn't make moving away from Raoul any easier, especially when he didn't seem disturbed by it at all.

They clinked their glasses together. "And to new beginnings," he said.

Her heart fluttered in spite of herself. "As in?"

"I'm expanding my diving and recovery operations."

"Great. That's just great." She didn't clink to that. In fact, she set her glass on the counter and turned away.

"I knew this wouldn't work," he said. "I gave romance a shot, but I knew I couldn't pull it off."

Tears welled in her eyes. She blinked hard, determined not to let Raoul see them. "You don't have to explain. Things are what they are."

"One more toast, Jaci."

"No, thanks. I've had all the celebration I can handle for one night."

"Just pick up the glass, please."

She turned around to tell him what he could do with his champagne and his new beginnings. He was down on one knee. Her heart jumped to her throat.

"The ring's in the bottom of the champagne flute. You were supposed to find it, throw your arms around me and say yes. But I guess I'll just beg the old-fashioned way. I know I'm ready now to fully go on with my life. I want passion. I want happiness. I want you. Marry me, Jaci. Marry me, and let me love you for the rest of our lives."

"Yes! Yes!" She started to throw her arms around him, but hesitated. "My job is in Miami."

"I know, and mine is all over the world. But I'm moving my headquarters to Miami. I didn't want to say anything until the plans were finalized. That's what I was doing the last two—"

She cut off his words by pressing her lips to his. The kiss was breathtaking, but she pulled away long before she'd had enough.

"I just have to make one quick phone call."

She dialed the number and waited for her mother to answer. "Can't make dinner, Mom, but just wanted to let you know that you don't have to worry about finding me a man anymore. In fact, you can go ahead and start planning my wedding."

"What did you say? Is this a joke? Is it that diver fellow? Have you set a date?"

Jaci didn't answer. She was already stepping out of her sexy black dress and getting ready for a celebration she'd remember for the rest of her wonderful, marvelous, passion-filled life.

Who said a woman forensics scientist couldn't have it all?

* * * * *

Set in darkness beyond the ordinary world.
Passionate tales of life and death.
With characters' lives ruled by laws the
everyday world can't begin to imagine.

Introducing NOCTURNE, *a spine-tingling new*
line from Silhouette Books.

The thrills and chills begin with
UNFORGIVEN by Lindsay McKenna

Plucked from the depths of hell, former military
sharpshooter Reno Manchahi was hired by the government to kill a thief, but he had a mission of his
own. Descended from a family of shape-shifters,
Reno vowed to get the revenge he'd thirsted for all
these years. But his mission went awry when his
target turned out to be a powerful seductress, Mag-
dalena Calen Hernandez, who risked everything to
battle a potent evil. Suddenly, Reno had to trans-
form himself into a true hero and fight the enemy
that threatened them all. He had to become a
Warrior for the Light....

Turn the page for a sneak preview of
UNFORGIVEN by Lindsay McKenna.
On sale September 26,
wherever books are sold.

Chapter 1

One shot...one kill.

The sixteen-pound sledgehammer came down with such fierce power that the granite boulder shattered instantly. A spray of glittering mica exploded into the air and sparkled momentarily around the man who wielded the tool as if it were a weapon. Sweat ran in rivulets down Reno Manchahi's drawn, intense face. Naked from the waist up, the hot July sun beating down on his back, he hefted the sledgehammer skyward once more. Muscles in his thick forearms leaped and biceps bulged. Even his breath was focused on the boulder. In his mind's eye, he pictured Army General Robert Hampton's fleshy, arrogant fifty-year-old features on the rock's surface. Air exploded from between his lips as he brought the avenging hammer down. The boulder pulverized beneath his funneled hatred.

One shot...one kill...

Nostrils flaring, he inhaled the dank, humid heat and drew it deep into his massive lungs. Revenge allowed Reno to endure his imprisonment at a U.S. Navy brig near San Diego, California. Drops of sweat were flung in all directions as the crack of his sledgehammer claimed a third stone victim. Mouth taut, Reno moved to the next boulder.

The other prisoners in the stone yard gave him a wide berth. They always did. They instinctively felt his simmering hatred, the palpable revenge in his cinnamon-colored eyes, was more than skin-deep.

And they whispered he was different.

Reno enjoyed being a loner for good reason. He came from a medicine family of shape-shifters. But even this secret power had not protected him—or his family. His wife, Ilona, and his three-year-old daughter, Sarah, were dead. Murdered by Army General Hampton in their former home on USMC base in Camp Pendleton, California. Bitterness thrummed through Reno as he savagely pushed the toe of his scarred leather boot against several smaller pieces of gray granite that were in his way.

The sun beat down upon Manchahi's naked shoulders, grown dark red over time, shouting his half-Apache heritage. With his straight black hair grazing his thick shoulders, copper skin and broad face with high cheekbones, everyone knew he was Indian. When he'd first arrived at the brig, some of the prisoners taunted him and called him Geronimo. Something strange happened to Reno during his fight with the name-calling prisoners. Leaning down after he'd won the scuffle, he'd snarled into each of their bloodied faces that if they were going to call him anything, they would call him *gan*, which was the Apache word for *devil*.

His attackers had been shocked by the wounds on their faces, the deep claw marks. Reno recalled doubling his fist as they'd attacked him en masse. In that split second, he'd gone into an altered state of consciousness. In times of danger, he transformed into a jaguar. A deep, growling sound had emitted from his throat as he defended himself in the three-against-one fracas. It all happened so fast that he thought he had imagined it. He'd seen his hands morph into a forearm and paw, claws extended. The slashes left on the three men's faces after the fight told him he'd begun to shape-shift. A fist made bruises and swelling; not four perfect, deep claw marks. Stunned and anxious, he hid the knowledge of what else he was from these prisoners. Reno's only defense was to make all the prisoners so damned scared of him and remain a loner.

Alone. Yeah, he was alone, all right. The steel hammer swept downward with hellish ferocity. As the granite groaned in protest, Reno shut his eyes for just a moment. Sweat dripped off his nose and square chin.

Straightening, he wiped his furrowed, wet brow and looked into the pale blue sky. What got his attention was the startling cry of a red-tailed hawk as it flew over the brig yard. Squinting, he watched the bird. Reno could make out the rust-colored tail on the hawk. As a kid growing up on the Apache reservation in Arizona, Reno knew that all animals that appeared before him were messengers.

Brother, what message do you bring me? Reno knew one had to ask in order to receive. Allowing the sledgehammer to drop to his side, he concentrated on the hawk who wheeled in tightening circles above him.

Freedom! the hawk cried in return.

Reno shook his head, his black hair moving against his broad, thickset shoulders. *Freedom? No way, Brother. No way.* Figuring that he was making up the hawk's shrill message, Reno turned away. Back to his rocks. Back to picturing Hampton's smug face.

Freedom!

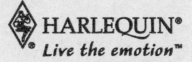

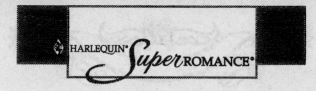
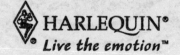

Harlequin Historicals®
Historical Romantic Adventure!

*From rugged lawmen and
valiant knights to defiant heiresses
and spirited frontierswomen,
Harlequin Historicals will
capture your imagination with
their dramatic scope, passion
and adventure.*

*Harlequin Historicals . . .
they're too good to miss!*

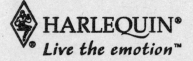